Sex and the Supernatural

Sex and the Supernatural

SEXUALITY IN RELIGION AND MAGIC

BENJAMIN WALKER

HARROW BOOKS
Harper & Row, Publishers
New York, Evanston, San Francisco, London

This book was originally published in England by Macdonald Unit 75. It is here reprinted by arrangement.

 For information address Ottenheimer Publishers Inc., 1632 Reisterstown Road at Naylors Lane, Baltimore, Maryland 21208. Published simultaneously in Canada by Fitzhenry & Whiteside Limited, Toronto.

First HARROW edition published 1973.

STANDARD BOOK NUMBER: 06-087043-5

Contents

1	The Emerald Tablet	7
2	The Prevalence of Sex	14
3	The Polarities	20
4	Woman as Mother and Witch	29
5	Man	40
6	The Succubus	44
7	Thought-Forms	57
8	The Puritan	69
9	Asceticism	75
10	A Brief History	89
	Further Reading	126

I

The Emerald Tablet

It is not necessary to understand the physics of a gun's mechanism, or the chemistry of the exploding bullet, in order to kill a man. A child could pull the trigger of a loaded revolver and do that.

The act of intercourse does not require an understanding of it, and men and women are drawn together without knowing the metaphysics of sex or the subtle alchemy that could transmute their union into a supernatural rite.

Yet there exists an age-old tradition known in many countries of the world about the hidden side of sex. Some of this curious lore survives as an inheritance handed down by word of mouth and still practised in secret cults, and a little, it seems almost inadvertently, has been put down in writing, scattered sparsely in rare books like small ingots that have accidentally fallen from the treasure of a caravan crossing a desert and lie half buried in the sand.

An ancient Chinese master used to say of his teachings that he revealed only one corner of the mystery; it was up to the pupil to discover the other three corners for himself, and something similar has been said by all who have discoursed on the subject. At the same time writers on sexual mysticism have warned of the dangers involved in becoming too inquisitive about this branch of hidden wisdom. Sex knowledge wrongly applied, said a Hindu sage, could interfere with the continuum of creation and bring on the final chaos. The Greeks of antiquity did not dabble much in sex as an occult study; Eros, they believed, was not a god to be trifled with. Jewish rabbis warned against attempting to probe too deeply into the sexual symbolism concealed in the early books of the Bible, for it was like bringing fire to flax.

In a modern scientific age such melodrama about sex, one of the most commonplace of animal activities, which any family physician will discuss without pretentiousness, and which is explained in full detail in scores of books readily obtainable in a public library, might strike one as rather ridiculous. What more is there to know about sex, and what is the purpose behind this insistence on caution and secrecy?

To understand this we must appreciate the fact that sex has not only its own physiology but also its own mysticism and its own mythology. Curiously enough a great deal of it is to be found in the Bible. The Book of Genesis in particular is regarded as a storehouse of secrets. It is claimed that far from being a legend about the creation of the world, it contains a profound symbolism which if properly understood would uncover the great mystery of existence itself. Its exposition has fostered an immense scholarship, first begun in the Hebrew *Talmud*, a weighty study of the Old Testament, and continued in part in the *Kabbalah*, a theosophy developed by the Jews of the Middle Ages; Christian scholars too have sought to unravel the tight skein that comprises the book, and all have claimed to have discovered an encyclopedia of meaning in the first few verses alone. St Jerome said that it contained as many secrets as syllables.

Genesis has been given in turn a symbolical, mystical, astrological, metaphysical and numerological interpretation. It is also said to have another hidden meaning, sexual in character. According to Madame Blavatsky, the founder of modern theosophy who, whatever her shortcomings might have been, was profoundly versed in occult matters, the early books of the Bible (the Pentateuch) were 'the symbolical narrative of the sexes, and an apotheosis of phallicism'.

It has, of course, also been given a literal interpretation. There are always pitfalls in the path of the fundamentalist who tries to attribute too precise a meaning to what is expressed in words, for the highest scriptures transcend their texts. But men have ever laboured to do honour to the written words of revelation. For example, the chronology of Genesis has been painstakingly worked backwards to arrive at a date for the primordial days. Bishop Usher of Armagh, in Ireland, in the middle of the 17th century, calculated that the creation of the world occurred in the year 4004 BC. About fifteen years later Dr John Lightfoot, Vice-Chancellor of Cambridge University, added the further interesting detail that man was created on 23 October of that year, 'at nine o'clock in the morning'. More than a century before their time, Martin Luther had already completed the sad tally of the Fall by pronouncing that Adam and Eve entered the garden at noon and partook of the apple 'at about two o'clock'.

Whatever we may think of this pious scholarship, it seems that Adam and Eve are permanent fixtures in the psyche of Christendom. They may belong to a non-existent period of remote dream-time, and Eden may be a legendary scene in another dimension, but along with the other great archetypes the tale of our first parents can be accepted without it compromising our integrity as intelligent post-Darwinian people.

But much else that belongs to the study of sex and the supernatural might be more difficult to swallow. Like other branches of the occult it draws on obsolete traditions kept alive by a zealous few, and in studying it we enter a strange world quite off the beaten track, whose unwritten annals go back to a period before the pages of accredited history to the shadowy past of the human race, and whose texts include not only the story of Adam and Eve but the great esoteric mythologies of Egypt, Babylonia, China, India, and Greece.

In spite of its overlay of superstition and credulity, many serious students are having increasing reservations about passing any drastic judgment on the ancient written and oral tradition that enshrines these beliefs. It has had a remarkable diffusion in the past, and commands an allegiance, and some might hope a diminishing one, among intelligent people even today. But it makes its appeal primarily to the subtle intuitions of the mind that lie below the threshold of the intellect, beyond any of the academic disciplines that are subject to the rules of reason and common sense.

The science-oriented man hates dogmas accepted

blindly, but here we have postulates that belong to fantasy, assumptions without proof or rational justification, and frequently beyond credence, and much that is altogether suggestive of hysteria and hallucination. If this is a lunacy of sorts it needs to be understood, if for no other reason than that it offers a fascinating field for the study of some of the most bizarre, if at times unwholesome, speculations of the human mind.

We live in a world most of which, in spite of our hopes and endeavours, might be said to be permanently outside the scope of our understanding. After science has had its innings in trying to interpret what the universe is about in terms of 'atoms and the void', 'matter and motion', and so on, there still remains a considerable residue that lies unexplained, and there is a growing realisation that the natural world cannot be understood within the context of observation and experiment, or grasped by means of the senses and reason. It continues to be an ever-expanding area of perplexity. We solve one problem only to be confronted with a dozen others more subtle than the one we have solved.

Things are not what they seem, and the apparent is only a distorted version of another reality. The ultimate principles of the world are very different from what we imagine them to be. Ludwig Wittgenstein (*d.* 1951), lecturer at the University of Cambridge, said unequivocally that 'the sense of the world must lie outside the world'. This is a philosopher's view, but the existence of two worlds and their close interrelationship is also the basic axiom of the supernatural. A mystical text known as the *Emerald Tablet* which enshrines some of the principles of occultism says, 'As above, so below', which again is almost pure Platonism. An implicit correspondence subsists between this world and 'that'.

Another postulate of the supernatural is that the world about us is fundamentally spiritual. Great thinkers even before Plato's time have stated the same thing in a hundred different ways. This concept of the 'other dimension' is central both to orthodox religious belief and to black magic. It has made strange bedfellows of the saint and the satanist. Again, the supernatural or spiritual world is of greater significance than the world we know through our senses. Man, like the great cosmic tree of so many mythologies, has his roots in another sphere, and with what faith he nourishes the spiritual roots, determines the fruit both here and hereafter.

It is as difficult to explain the interconnection of the two worlds as it is to demonstrate the stages linking the cerebral cortex and the process called thinking. How does a physical nerve impulse cause an idea to come into being? What has the lump of 'repulsive matter' known as the brain got in common with a musical fugue or a mystical experience? However much we shake a dead brain we cannot produce that intangible, non-dimensional 'illumination' we call a thought. These platitudes underlie the enigma of that elusive point where two worlds intersect, and the ramifications of the hidden channels that connect the individual founts of our being with the great cosmic ocean beyond.

It will be clear, then, that if we wish to trace the

tenuous connection between sex and the supernatural we must be moved by a spirit of understanding, 'suspend disbelief' and taking the absurd in our stride, enter willingly into the realm of mystification. And this may be difficult unless we acquire the knack, like the Queen in *Alice*, of being able to believe six impossible things before breakfast.

2

The Prevalence of Sex

A FAMOUS 18th-century Irish philosopher, Bishop Berkeley, had a theory, one interpretation of which is that the world exists only because there is a Perceiver who upholds it by His perception. God looks on, and the world is sustained. If He turned away or withdrew His cognizance of the world then, as Berkeley put it, 'all the choir of heaven and furniture of earth which compose the mighty frame of the world', would vanish into nothingness.

One medieval school of Jewish kabbalists taught that all creation is upheld by sexual activity. Stop it, and the universe will slowly dissolve like a salt castle immersed in a running stream.

The coming together of man and woman in the act of intimate union has inspired some of the most extraordinary beliefs of mankind. At one extreme we find those who in a paradoxical reaction from its influence have held that sexual activity is a source of spiritual danger and moral corruption and that sex is responsible for man's damnation; and at the other extreme, those who use sex as a means for attaining the highest mystical experience and gaining an awareness of the hidden truths of the universe, and who preach salvation through sex.

From earliest times sexual union has been sanctified in countless symbols, and the representation of the act was a profound arcanum concealing hidden truths. The Ark of the Covenant, the chest of acacia wood housed in the Holy of Holies in the Temple of Solomon, contained among other things a sacred stone which, according to certain Talmudic scholars, was a symbol of the male and female organs in union. The Eleusinian mysteries of ancient Greece included a rite known as *arretophoria* named from the Greek words meaning 'carrying things not to be mentioned', in which a basket containing a stone phallus and the 'womb' of the goddess Demeter was taken out in sacred procession.

In primitive (preliterate) societies it was and still is almost universally believed that human generation is directly linked with supernatural powers. Even in those communities – and there are some, according to anthropologists – who are not aware of the connection between sexual intercourse and pregnancy, the act of copulation takes on a special significance and is regarded with sentiments of religious awe.

The history of sex in religious rites is almost coterminous with man. The all-pervasive nature of the sex instinct, its imperious demands, its mystery, its pleasures, brought it early within the ambit of man's religious ceremonial. The miraculous nature of the gift of sex must have appeared almost magical to the primitive mind, as indeed it often does to the civilised. Legends and folk-tales of all nations are filled with allusions to sex. Phallic emblems, sacred prostitution, fertility rites, marriage customs, all sprang from it.

Ancient Egyptian worship had a vast eroticism, which is seen in its extreme form in the phallicism of the Osiris cult and ritual bestiality. More than one festive pageant of the ancient world included the phallephoria, or phallus-bearers, who carried huge reproductions of the male organ on long poles, which they set in motion by pulling strings. This was not a piece of obscenity but an act of religious import.

The Hindu religion bears striking evidence of sexual symbolism, which reached its apotheosis in the worship of the *linga* or phallus of the god Shiva. Much of Hindu temple art is distinctly phallic, and has its textual parallel in the Vedas, the Upanishads and others of their sacred writings, where the sexual and divine are closely equated. Religious sculptures in Africa, South America, China, and Japan also emphasise the intimate relationship between piety and sex. Furthermore, in Christian church architecture the various structural features, from the steeple aspiring upwards, to the formal plan of the interior, the columns, vestibule, pulpit, and altar, have all been ascribed a phallic significance by some authorities. The medieval church grotesques sculptured both inside and out were at times overtly lewd. Priapus entered Christianity in the guise of certain saints who were venerated in forms that left no doubt as to their antecedents. The very word veneration is said to be derived from the name of the sex-goddess Venus.

Sexuality as an operative and active agent has pervaded every facet of human life and conduct, and its symbolism is universal. All projections and convexities suggest the male attributes, all depressions and concavities the female. This is not a Freudian discovery but an association as old as history and as widespread as man. There is hardly an object, an incident, a legend, a natural or biological phenomenon that has not through the ages reminded man of the reproductive organs, the female form, or the sexual act, and their concomitants: erection, coition, emission, pregnancy, parturition.

There is no limit to sexual symbolism. The upreared hills, the fertile valleys, gushing waterfalls, and mountain torrents; birds that fly in the air, fish that swim in the sea, sleek animals that roam the earth, the phallic snake, and the smooth shell with its pink interior: all evoke their sexual equivalence.

Seasonal rites connected with ploughing, sowing, reaping, and harvesting were associated with sex and magic. Apart from the concept of fertility, which was naturally sexual in character, the peoples of antiquity ascribed a gender to all nature, including atmospheric and cosmic phenomena. The sky was the father god who in the form of rain fertilised mother earth, and most rain-making ceremonies throughout the world had a sexual element in them.

Ploughing the field was the ceremony of opening and preparing the earth to receive the seed that was going to be planted within its womb. The agricultural implements were dubbed with appropriate appellations to designate their part in a sexual performance; the plough was the phallus, the furrow the woman. At the time of sowing the process was often mimetically enacted by the community as a religious rite, in which men and women would perform the act of intercourse in the open field so as to inspire the earth and sky to abundance and increase. 'As above, so below', as the Emerald Tablet expressed it. And these rites were not, as might be supposed, confined to remote or backward communities, but prevailed until recently in western countries as well. Until the beginning of the present century peasants in parts of Europe used to have intercourse with their wives in the fields after sowing, to ensure a good crop.

Sexual activity, it was thought, relaxes the stringency of the divine dispensation in heaven. Hence the aborigines of Australia, when threatened by a storm or the ominous *aurora australis*, indulged in promiscuous sexual intercourse in order to relieve the tensions 'up there'. On the same principle the people of Patagonia, when faced with a season of misfortune, would send their wives elsewhere to yield themselves to the first stranger they met. And in the ancient Middle East, especially in Canaan, temple worship was frequently linked with the dedication of phallic energy, blood, and other bodily excretions as an offering to the deities in return for their favours. An incident recorded by the Greeks tells us that when the Locrians of Magna Graecia found themselves in trouble with their powerful neighbours they proposed to avert disaster by placing their wives in the city brothels for one month.

Together with the idea of the universal prevalence of gender, a belief in the supernatural world and the interconnectedness of things is part of primitive man's magical inheritance. For him the two worlds merge:

heaven and earth are united; everything is supernatural, and the whole universe is vibrant with an animating presence. Mimetic actions performed in this world cause changes in the other world.

Some vestige of these primordial beliefs seems to underlie the conviction of the sex magician. To him also there is a vast interpenetration of the two spheres, and the power engendered by sexual ritual performed in a prescribed manner in the one sphere is able to induce a corresponding activity in the other. Sex, therefore, can become a channel for the direct experience of the supernatural.

3
The Polarities

A BASIC gender is inherent in all phenomena. A polarity runs through the world, for every entity needs an opposite. An English poet and mystic said, 'Without contraries is no progression', and a German philosopher, 'A thing can only exist through its contrary'. But long before Blake and Hegel the ancients had come to recognise and accept the identical concept.

Except the Godhead, who is Absolute and hence all-sufficing, a unity remains neutral and inoperative. An opposite exists in everything, and oppositeness lies at the foundation of existence itself. A vast metaphysical system has arisen on the basis of the essential two-ness of the world. The Zoroastrians of ancient Persia were the first to give the two opposing principles a theistic signification as the Powers of Good and Evil, and since their time dualism has run like a red thread through religious thought. Embellished further by the Persian reformer, Mani of Ecbatana (*d.* AD 276), the idea found its way into the Christian stream and profoundly influenced St Augustine before his conversion, but met with outright condemnation from the theologians, who denounced Zoroaster as the patriarch of diabolism and founder of the black arts, for putting, as they thought he did, God and the Devil on an equal footing.

This seeming rigmarole of philosophy is a necessary digression, and one of profound importance to the understanding of our subject, for several minor patterns relating to sex and the supernatural have been woven into the fabric of the dualistic theory. One concerns man and his opposite – woman. The second concerns man and the opposite within himself. Elements of the first may be discerned in Plato's *Symposium* where it is said that in the beginning male and female were halves of a primordial androgyne (man-woman) which had existed in united form and afterwards divided. The notion of such a 'splitting' underlies the meaning of the word *sex*, for sex simply means 'division'.

A similar idea appears in one interpretation of the Garden of Eden story, in which Adam is described as an hermaphrodite being a single whole comprising both male and female. Eve was created from his flesh. Like Platonic man, Edenic man 'split' to form his helpmeet. Variations of this legend occur in Hinduism and several other mythologies of the world.

As halves we seek to be made whole. The mutual attraction of the sexes is the craving of an incomplete being to be made complete. And the delight that comes from having found one's opposite half is love; and the pleasure that comes from uniting with that half, each mutually assuaging the other's ache, is sexual pleasure. The sexual act restores the original oneness of the human being.

Besides the differences of genders as exemplified in

the two sexes, male and female, there exists an oppositeness within each individual, dividing one side from another side within himself. Just as there was within the original Adam a complete being Adam-Eve, so there is within each person a duality, a positive and negative polarity which ramifies through the physiological, mental and psychical planes that constitute his identity.

Definitions of precisely what these polar opposites are vary with different theories. In one, the right and left sides of man are the two poles whose opposing potencies proliferate through the body and provide the magnetic field that is responsible for his vitality and existence. The right and left nostrils according to yogic teachings are channels for two distinct kinds of breath, oppositely charged. The cerebral plexus connected with the diaphragm, or the solar plexus with the heart, each creates its own circuit and carries its own peculiar current of power. In yoga all such unions entail a specialised study requiring years to master, and yogic manuals promise all kinds of magical powers to the successful aspirant of these processes of self-conjugation.

Especially important for the purpose of sex magic is one particular set of opposites whose union sends an unparalleled surge of vital energy through the whole frame, namely, the lungs and the testes. This is one of the great arcana of sex mysticism. Its goal lies in the fusion, through the corporeal vehicles of the lungs and the testes, of the subtle forces immanent in breath and semen. A massive written and oral tradition on the mystique of breath has been handed down from ancient times, and the understanding of this dual mystery of respiration and the seminal essence forms an intrinsic part of the science of sex magic. We shall touch on it briefly again when we deal with the Taoist system of China.

The individual whose inner opposites are still quiescent is regarded as potentially explosive to a high degree. The arc of his power has not yet formed a circuit and there is, it is believed, always a searing flash when the energy crosses over. The two exemplars of such types of person are the adolescent and the virgin.

Puberty is one of the landmarks in the life-cycle of every man. At this time the equilibrium of forces within him begins to tremble into imbalance, and stability can only be restored on the higher level of adulthood and maturity. A strange effervescence bubbles in the blood and sends forth a ferment that transmutes the body. If people can get drunk on alcohol why not on the more potent intoxicant of the internal secretions that are being engendered within the body, causing the breasts of the young girl to blossom and giving the boy a heavier voice and putting hair on his chin and chest? And with them come strange surgings lower down; unaccountable feelings from the psychohormones that blaze through the arteries and fire the flesh.

It is a dangerous time, full of pitfalls for the individual as well as for the community. It was thought that the young could never achieve the tranquillity necessary for responsible behaviour; that they could no more stop their ebullience than the tree could prevent the sap from rising in spring. Hence societies, especially tribal peoples, have felt the need to harness and if need be to choke the gushing springs of adolescence by subjecting them to harsh discipline lest they burst forth unchecked and inundate the community.

Youth is a supernatural time. Hence many occult and religious observances call for youthful participants. They seem to stimulate the psychic atmosphere and send an irradiance into the spiritual realms. According to psychical research their presence often triggers paranormal manifestations, and the phenomenon of poltergeists, for instance, apparently needs their particular kind of pubescent energy to produce its physical effects. Virgin girls seem to be especially responsive to the overtones of a psychic atmosphere.

The subject of virginity and defloration is hedged in by stringent taboos in many parts of the world, and the fact of a man having illicit intercourse with a virgin arouses deep-seated emotions, as though some sacred prohibition has been outraged. Even in the more permissive societies of the western world it still holds a place among the last of the surviving sex taboos, and the rape of a girl ranks as what used to be known as a felonious act, and is regarded as deserving of severe legal reprisal.

According to an earlier belief common to many nations, the illicit ravishing of a maiden, whether with or without her consent, caused both parties to suffer irreparable psychic injury, and so special measures were taken to ward off the evils and dangers believed to accompany defloration. Certain peoples imagined that a serpent lay in wait in the vagina and bit the first male organ that entered; others believed that hymenal blood was a virulent poison whose evil power ruined a man's erectile capability. In ancient Babylon virgin girls gave themselves to strangers within the sacred temple precincts and only then returned home to settle down safely to a respectable married life. Hindu girls used to be deflowered on a stone appropriately shaped and set up in a corner of the temple shrine. For the same reason Roman brides, just before entering the marital chamber, were made to squat on the lap of a statue of the ithyphallic god Mutunus Tutunus.

In many parts of the world, including western Christendom, the act of defloration was carried out by a personage (priest, king, seigneur) sufficiently exalted to withstand the charge of power that was thought to follow its accomplishment, or else by a man (the husband) who was sanctified by the rite of marriage and immunised, so to speak, against its impact.

The Hindu sage, Shvetaketu, held that a promiscuous society that permitted the violation of virgins with impunity was a sure invitation to national disaster. Prosperous kingdoms came to their end not because they were corrupted by luxury but because their disregard for the sanctity of the virgin knot removed the protective barriers against the invasion of destructive forces from the unseen world.

So strong was the taboo against taking the life of a virgin, except as a sacrifice to the deities, that in some places special legislation was passed on their behalf. In Rome virgins could not be made to suffer capital punishment. If a Vestal were found guilty of an indiscretion affecting her virgin status she was taken in solemn procession to a place near the Colline Gate and entombed alive in a special underground chamber, along with sufficient food to last her a few days. She was then regarded as having starved to death, so that the onus of her death did not rest on the state or prejudice the welfare of its citizens.

What was likely to happen to a secular virgin condemned to death may be judged from the story related about Sejanus, a minister of the Roman emperor Tiberius, who was convicted for treachery. The minister and his family were sentenced to death. But the family included a virgin daughter who by the laws of the land could not be executed. The emperor therefore gave orders for the girl to be raped by the executioner first, and then strangled. And this was done.

In European society depucellement was for centuries conventionally counted as one of the privileges of ownership linked with feudal rights, where the authority of the seigneur included the right to the maidenhead of the brides of all vassals under fealty to him. Historical evidence suggests that the seigneurs sometimes exercised their prerogative.

Defloration mania appears as a recurrent motif in the social history of Europe and the demand for intact girls of tender age grew into a pathological obsession among the higher classes in 18th-century England. Men proved their virility by boasting of their conquests. One mentally deformed gallant proudly claimed that he was responsible for the debauching of seventy girls in a single year, and others of his sick brigade tried to equal the score. Exclusive clubs were formed to provide the girls, many of them of a diabolist nature, appropriately labelled Hellfire Clubs. Besides the usual drunkenness and wenching that were the regular features of their meetings, there were blasphemies against the Holy Ghost, formal pacts with the devil, the ritual rape of virgin victims, and sex acts some of which required three or more participants operating simultaneously.

London continued to be the centre of the craze for virgins until the last decades of the 19th century. When W. T. Stead, editor of the *Pall Mall Gazette*, investigated the situation in the 'Modern Babylon', he found that the sale of girls, some of them thirteen years old, was more widespread in prim Victorian England than most people would have believed possible. Since demand frequently exceeded supply there was a lucrative trade in the commodity, and reconditioned 'virgins' duly patched up with chicken-skin, rubber strips and other expedients were put on the market over and over again.

What lies behind the mystique of virginity? And behind the mania for defloration in particular? In the marriage market, of course, the idea prevails that an intact bride represents a guarantee of unviolated property, but this is a comparatively late rationalisation of a requirement that was in fact confined only to a few societies. The presence of the membrane does not provide conclusive proof of untouched property, and damaged goods can be mended with a little skill. Nor does its absence invariably indicate that the girl has lost her virgin status.

Secondly, there is the thrill of the pioneering male, opening the secret springs of life for the first time and initiating the innocent girl into the mysteries of sex. There is also the sadistic instinct to inflict pain which some men are only too glad to express in this manner. Pornographic literature frequently dwells with zest on the lecher tormenting and humiliating some hapless maiden, laughing at her cries for help and mocking at her pleas for mercy, before he 'ravishes' or 'violates' her. It all adds to his fun, as well as the reader's. Then we have the old superstition that sexual intercourse with a virgin will cure venereal disease, an abominable idea that is still rife, even in civilised countries. Again, there is the equally tenacious belief in the rejuvenative value of shed blood, which in this case directly laves the organ in need of the restorative.

But there is yet another, a magical concept of virginity with a long folkloric and occult history. The virgin is a replica of Adam-Eve, the sinless one in the garden of Eden. In folk etymology the word virgin comes from *vir-gyne,* 'man-woman', a whole, intact person. Girls before carnal knowledge were therefore thought to have a peculiar ability to control nature, such as Adam possessed before the Fall.

To the practitioner of the black arts virginity is a force as potent as a bent bow, an untapped source of occult energy. By means of a secret rite he breaks into the interior places of the virgin for the first time and releases the unexpended energy, utilising it to recharge himself with power, at the same time making an oblation to the deities to whom his rite is dedicated.

4

Woman as Mother and Witch

THERE is a mystery about womankind. Such a statement presupposes the masculine viewpoint. But although it is the man talking, his attitude, it will be claimed by him, is not part of a masculine pretence but an opinion sincerely held, for not many men presume to understand the opposite sex. Tolstoy, one of the few who did have a profound insight into the workings of the female mind, was once heard to remark, 'I am only going to tell the truth about women when I have one foot in the grave. I shall say it, jump into the coffin and pull down the lid.'

Some women seem to be conscious of their mystery as well, but as Kant said, they 'don't give their secret away'. Precisely wherein the secret lies perhaps most women do not know themselves, or do not care to know, as long as they know they have it.

Those who have given some thought to the matter have come to the conclusion that fundamentally, and in spite of all physical intimacies, woman remains inaccessible to the male. From the time he dwelt in caves man has thrown up his hands in despair trying to fathom this weeping and stoical, cowardly and heroic, complaining and enduring, comforting and infuriating helpmeet that the gods have provided for his solace and martyrdom.

The behaviour, appearance, and above all the physiological life of woman have ever dominated the curiosity and imagination of the male. Schopenhauer had harsh words for the 'undersized, narrow-shouldered, broad-hipped, short-legged, long-torsoed, teat-bedecked creature' which, he said, only the male befogged by the sexual urge could regard as beautiful. But Schopenhauer was not the best authority on the subject, and most men from infancy onwards have been irresistibly drawn to the warmth of her breasts and the consolation of her arms. Man's understanding of woman, as wife and mother, is reflected in the words of poets, whose songs in her praise often surpass in beauty and tenderness the hymns written in praise of God.

But the mystique of woman as the object of romantic affection has a dark and inversive side, and is not incompatible with the idea of woman as a taboo, and a danger to be avoided. Her sex both exalts and debases her. She attracts and repels; she is pursued and shunned; feared as much as desired.

No less bewildering to herself than it is disturbing to the male are the physiological changes peculiar to her sex. From menses to menopause her experiences are a series of painful crises. She is nature's masochist, created to bear, and hence liable to attract, trouble.

First comes the onset of puberty with its menstrual flow each month. Primitive communities avoided the impure presence of the menstruating woman who was believed to contaminate on sight, and she was confined to special quarters and cut off from normal human contact until the period was over. Again, a girl's first experience with the opposite sex is usually one of pain and blood, not to mention the other psychical concomitants that are thought to arise from the encounter, as we have seen. Then comes the crucial period of pregnancy which, some think, hideously deforms her, gives her an ugly waddling gait, provokes capricious appetites and bizarre changes of mood, and prepares her for another animal purpose – lactation.

Finally there is the upheaval of parturition. That childbirth was indeed a calamity was an idea held by quite a number of sects some of which played an important part in religious history. The Cathars, for instance, believed that a pregnant woman carried the devil in her. They interpreted the verse in Genesis 3.16 to read: 'Thou shalt bring forth children in evilness' (instead of 'sorrow'). Man, they said, is conceived in base desires, born of brutish urges and animal postures, encased for nine months in the body of an unclean creature, and expelled from the womb in a cataract of blood, mucus, and dead tissue. Pliny the Roman orator said, 'It is humiliating to the pride of man to consider the pitiable origin of this most arrogant of creatures'. The philosopher, Kierkegaard, declared that it was an abominable lie to say that marriage pleased God. From the Christian standpoint it was a crime, made worse because it brought innocent individuals into existence.

Again in the male-female association it is almost invariably the woman who is maligned. She is the evil genius of the partnership. She is sex incarnate and sex is of the devil. Sin and woman are synonymous. This view was not that of a misogynist sect or an eccentric philosopher but one that was affirmed by almost every major religion.

'Women,' say the Arabs, 'are the whips of Satan.' 'There are seven kinds of poisons,' says a Hindu text, 'and the most venomous is woman.' 'Woman is an unavoidable calamity,' said St Chrysostom. 'A tool of Satan and the pathway to hell,' said St Jerome. The Indian epic, *Mahabharata,* adds this verdict to the general consensus: 'A man with a hundred tongues who lives for a hundred years would not be able to describe completely the vices and defects of a woman.'

In Buddhist religious manuals meant for the monastic orders the prohibitions against too close an association with the opposite sex might be summarised, in order of increasing restriction, somewhat as follows: avoid sexual intercourse; do not have any physical contact with women; do not talk to them; avoid company where women are present; do not look in their direction; do not look at sculptural or pictorial representations of women; do not read about them; do not talk about them; do not wish for them; banish them from your thoughts. When Buddha was asked by one of his disciples how he should behave towards women he said, 'Do not see them, Ananda. If you have to see them abstain from speech, Ananda. If you should speak to them, keep wide awake, Ananda!'

Even in our modern age the slander of women has not entirely abated and to many men feminism still spells one of mankind's great disasters. In the folklore of the sexes the woman fares just as badly. She is the deadlier of the two. The man is of as little consequence as the male of the praying mantis or a species of spider, who cautiously approaches his mate, hurriedly performs the act, and scurries off if he can manage it. Because more often than not once his part is over, and sometimes even while he is engaged in the fulfilment of the creative urge, the female nips off his head and then feasts at leisure on the remains.

This devouring-female image often haunts the nightmares of neurotics, and is not uncommon in various guises in the ordinary dreams of the average man. To a boy unused to the nude female figure his first sight of her vast undergrowth, and the thought of what lurks beyond can be a matter of frightening curiosity. The *vagina dentata*, the toothed vulva, waiting with cruel jaws like some beast of prey, is a well-known psychological symbol of the male's concern for his own virility when in the presence of the castrating and devirilising female.

Within the cavern of the vagina itself lies that other creature, the 'womb', and the womb too has become associated with some curious lore. There is a 'thing' within the womb, a being with a life of its own, that rages if not appeased. It was believed, in Greece for instance, that if the womb were overwrought, disturbed, angry, or unsatisfied, it would become restless and start moving about the body, causing the malady known as hysteria, which gets its name from the Greek word *hystera*, meaning womb. The Book of Proverbs speaks of the grave and the womb being equally insatiable. They never say, 'We have had enough'.

The legend of Pandora and her box is supposed to allude, among other things, to the evils arising out of the sexual curiosity of woman, her increased sexual knowledge, and her insatiable appetite. Once aroused, a woman grows by what she feeds upon. The ancient sage Tiresias, who had once been magically changed into a woman and lived as one for seven years, was asked by Jupiter which of the two sexes had the greater pleasure from intercourse. He replied that the woman enjoyed the act ten times more than the man, whereupon the goddess Juno, probably feeling that he had betrayed one of the secrets derogatory to her sex, blinded the candid sage. A similar story also occurs in Indian mythology, and in the Hindu account woman is compared to a dangerous pet that must be kept securely tethered to its post.

Altogether, in matters of sex expression a woman was not to be allowed full freedom. Her role was that of a passive vessel for the pleasure of the male, since she was created to give and not to take. 'A lady,' stated one of the Victorian dicta, 'does not shake.' In the cynic's view emancipation has now ordained not only that woman shake but that man be competent enough to provoke the activity to her satisfaction. Her own uninhibited movements might evoke more than a suspicion in her lover's mind of that demonism that the Church Fathers hinted at; and her powerful contractions might suggest a vampirism by which she would engulf and engorge the male member. If the man today seeks a docile vessel with whom he can cope in his own timid way, he will have to look elsewhere than among the Amazons of the permissive age. Modern man under the redoubtable matriarchs will become like the nervous spider, afraid to unbutton his pants.

But perhaps by then woman will have come into her own – the Great Mother and the Great Witch.

Woman is the magical bond between two worlds. Her function is not primarily sexual but supernatural. As the Great Mother she looms among the primeval archetypes and is invested with a frightening prestige. As though to emphasise her predominance, prehistoric man depicts her in a grotesque caricature of womanhood. Her breasts reach down to her knees, her gargantuan hips almost preclude penetration, her outline is a squat ovoid. But she is the ovoid that includes all, the shape that takes in everything. She is the Omniverse. Within the crucible of her being the great transmutations are achieved.

Through woman, too, the magical world is defined. She is the gateway to the mysteries and in almost every one of the world's great mystery religions she plays a leading role, as sibyl, pythia, or high priestess. Her function is paramount in all cults connected with sex. In Chinese Taoism women are among the greatest adepts of sex magic, and a number of Chinese classics on erotic mysticism are attributed to them. In India renowned tantriks have been tutored by crones adept in all forms of thaumaturgy. The *dakinis* who lead the Tibetan sorcerers through their necromantic initiations are primordial female beings having a knowledge of secret matters hidden from men. Similarly, witchcraft in medieval Europe was essentially a female business, and the patrons of the craft, apart from Satan himself, were Diana, Habundia, Salome, Herodias, all women. The term 'witch' is still popularly confined to the female.

From ancient times there have been cults and societies that have had an exclusively female membership, and several festivals were attended by women alone. The descriptions that survive of what went on suggest a form of sex worship so frenzied in character as to make it unsafe for any man to be in the vicinity.

The existence of such sororities may have given rise to the legends of larger female communities ruled by queens. From the Greeks we have several accounts of the warrior-women known as the Amazons who lived near the Caucasus or the borders of Persia. They were not celibate but as a rule selected their men from outside the community. Sometimes they broke one of the legs of their chosen captives, for, according to an Amazon princess, 'the lame best perform the act of love'. The strain that a limp puts on the crotch of a man was believed to strengthen the male organ. Whatever it was, the male selected for the privilege of intercourse with an Amazon could not have welcomed the favour. Even the fierce Scythians were afraid to approach their encampments lest they be overwhelmed, as it was customary for the girls to kill a man to prove their worth as warriors. It is conceivable that necrophilic rites were also practiced, a probability that may be further deduced from the incident recorded in Greek myth where Achilles had intercourse with the corpse of the Amazon queen Penthesilia after he had slain her.

From eastern records also we hear of the existence of several 'women's kingdoms'. Here again we come across organised communities, with women predominating. One such kingdom, Udyana, was a place of some notoriety according to the Hindu chronicles, where intercourse was regarded not only as a procreative act but was also used, in all its variations, for the acquisition of magical power. Their orgies specialised in magical sex-postures, each posture forming a mould for the capture of an occult force, by methods that cannot be described.

In the higher reaches of tantrism and other forms of left-hand occultism the presence of woman is imperative, and union with her provides the occasion and the means for contact with the other planes. The magician needs a counterpart or sexual opposite to make him whole and render him operative, and no successful result is possible without her. To a large extent this holds true even in many lower forms of malefic magic where occult potencies are best obtained through the talismanic charge drawn from the woman in ritual circumstances.

The great sexualised sects of India and Tibet provide each god with a female counterpart and depict the pair in union, and down the scale the hierophants serving the deities equip themselves likewise with female partners. All the great warlocks of the western tradition, too, depended for their effectiveness on women: from the sorcerer Simon Magus, mentioned in the Acts of the Apostles, whose counterpart Helen was essential for his operations, to Crowley who had a dynastic line of 'scarlet women' through whom his power was formulated.

It is important to realise in the understanding of sex in magic that its role is not basically voluptuary. The body and the particular parts of the women are employed 'dispassionately' as it were, without the erotic element predominating. In fact, in order to obviate any possibility of falling into the meshes of carnality, the true adept made sure that his counterpart was not the sort of woman to excite his sexual appetite.

In the context of sex magic, beauty is a snare and an impediment, for then the element of personal desire enters into what must be a dedicated religious rite. Physical charm can vitiate the efficacy of sexual magic. Hence the counterparts of most exponents of the magical tradition were unprepossessing. The tantrik sought his shakti or female opposite in a woman who belonged to the lowest caste, frequently a discarded prostitute lacking in all feminine attraction. The initiating crones of Vajrayana Buddhism have the 'marks of ugliness' to confirm their status. In seeking to enlarge his own tantrik-oriented experiences Crowley advertised for females of all kinds, deformed women, dwarfs, hunchbacks, and as he put it in his characteristically unfeeling way, 'freaks of all sorts'.

The purpose of such a choice by the magician is that with the 'accidents' of sensual allure removed, woman might fitly represent what she was meant to be in absolute terms – one totally other – the Vulva incarnate, unrelated to status, wealth, youthfulness, beauty, desire, pleasure, or procreation.

As a result of the legacy bequeathed by Eve, woman

fulfils every magical requirement, and through her the fruit of preternatural knowledge may be culled so that man and woman participating in a mystical rite might, in a satanic dispensation, and in Satan's words, 'be as gods'.

5
Man

MEN have been created because they are necessary for the gods. This idea, as old as ancient Sumeria, survived till the Middle Ages with a slight shift of emphasis, and is with us still. 'Man,' said Peter Lombard, 12th-century bishop of Paris, 'is made to serve God. The universe is made to serve man. Man is placed at the middle point of the universe, that he may both serve and be served.'

From the time when man first tried to establish his place in the universal order he believed himself to be the centre of things. The sun revolved around the earth, and he was the king of created beings. Aristarchus of Samos (*d.* 264 BC) was one of the first to propound the revolutionary heliocentric theory, maintaining that what lay at the centre of the universe was not the earth but the sun. No one paid much attention to Aristarchus until eighteen hundred years later when Copernicus in the 16th century put the theory on scientific lines and thus ended the priority of our planet in the hierarchy of celestial bodies.

But even though the earth was displaced from its central position man had the consolation of knowing that he was still the ruler of the earth, a unique being especially created by the Lord God in His own image. Until Darwin and his followers put the quietus on his arrogance. Man, it turned out, was the end product of a long process of evolution that began some millions of years ago from protoplasmic slime. In many ways several varieties of reptiles and worms are better adapted for life on earth than man is, and he is as likely to be snuffed out of existence as the mammoth and the sabre-toothed tiger.

Against this dispiriting theory we are offered another postulate – a dogma, both pre-Copernican and pre-Darwinian, yet not obsolete, for it is the rock on which the religious tradition stands. Regardless of what the astronomers have to say the earth, far from being an infinitesimal mote in the cloud-dust of the cosmos, is the very heart of the natural plenum. In spite of Darwin and the others man is, in fact, the hub of the universe. Around him revolves the whole of creation. For human existence is a happening in which divinity has directly intervened. Against the textbooks of science, the ancient myths and revealed scriptures of the various religions are brought forward. For the Jewish-Christian world some support of this contention is found in the Bible, that venerable patriarch among books which in whole or in part has brooded over the spiritual development of mankind for more than thirty centuries.

Medieval though it be, and relegated by science to the scrap-heap of other outmoded superstitions, yet this is what the idea implies: a belief in man that is almost rhapsodic.

Man, we are told, is a replica of a divine prototype and the universe is reflected in him. He is the centre of all the mysteries of heaven and earth and the abyss under the earth. 'Before man's spirit took bodily form,' said Plato, 'he lived among the gods in the spiritual realms.' In essence, man is a supernatural being. The Egyptians thought so. The Greeks thought so. So did the Chinese and Hindus. The *Zohar*, a kabbalistic treatise, says: 'As soon as man appeared all was achieved, both in the upper and lower worlds. For all is contained in man.' Although subject to the law of the flesh the human being, as St Paul says, is the citizen of another kingdom. He stands at the crossroads of two worlds and partakes of both dimensions. The earth's abundance is his birthright provided for his benefit.

His body is a mystery, his actions a trail of wonders. His thoughts are radiances, creative and dynamic. No other creature stands four-square to the world as he does. His gestures are linked to the movements of the constellations. His voice carries past the farthest stars to the throne of heaven. His face is a replica of the empyrean and on his body are secret signs limned from the stars. And through the chords of his being the music of the spheres sends forth its celestial diapason.

As long as he lives man retains the divine aroma breathed into his nostrils by the Almighty. The arrangement of his limbs is a special dispensation of God; the position of his sexual organs is part of the divine geometry. His creative apparatus represents not an animal appendage meant only for propagation but a magical instrument of transcendent power. It is the secret lamp of Aladdin and the transmuting stone of the philosophers. The *Kabbalah* describes the phallus as 'many worlds in length, erect over all things'.

The sex organs are a minicosm within the microcosm that is man. They constitute an arcane weapon wielded for creation and contact with the other realms. They lie ensconced in a magical area, and through sexual activity a divine mystery is enacted. Sexual union is a sacrament. It is so within the Roman Church when sanctified by marriage. Muslims and Zoroastrians are enjoined to utter a silent prayer before intercourse for it is consummated in the presence of God who has provided the pleasures that accompany it and furnished the blessings that follow its fulfilment. It is God's supreme will that man and woman should come together in the sacred union of the sexual act. A rabbi of the Hassidic sect of Jews said, 'God Himself decorated Eve's hair, so that she might please Adam more.'

And that brings us to the primary postulate of sex and the supernatural: that sex is not just a buzz in the genitals, or a form of biophysical electricity streaming through the flesh, but an occult power, attuned by invisible strings to the resounding harmonies of the cosmos.

6

The Succubus

THERE has always been a strong ambivalence in man's attitude to sex, and his opinions have moved from one extreme to another. Against the megalomania of the mystic with his ecstatic concept of man and his central place in the universe, and sex and its central place in man, we have therefore to set the opposite view.

It is a comparatively simple matter to dismiss the supernaturalism of sex in terms of physics and biology. Man then becomes merely an extension of the animal kingdom, reacting to the presence of the opposite sex like Pavlov's dogs salivating at the sound of a bell. Marriage becomes a social convenience, virginity an obstructive membrane, orgasm a spastic frenzy, and the whole panorama of sex, in the words of a Hindu Ajivika philosopher, of no more significance than 'squeezing a boil'.

The mystery of intercourse both fascinates and repels, and in considering it men have tended to be drawn in opposite emotional directions. It has as often been called a curse as a blessing. Plato records the reply given by the aged Sophocles when he was asked whether he still enjoyed the pleasures of sex. 'Hush sir,' said the poet, 'it gives me the greatest joy to have escaped from the clutches of that ravening monster.' Indeed, the famous Church Father, Origen (*d.* AD 257), felt the burden of sexual desire to be such a hindrance to the holy life that he castrated himself. He regretfully observed that but for their sin Adam and Eve would have propagated not by sexual union but in some 'mysterious angelic manner'.

Sir Thomas Browne (*d.* 1682), one of the most temperate and rational men of his time, expressed a similar sentiment. 'I could be content,' he wrote, 'that we might procreate like trees, without conjunction, or that there were any way to perpetuate the world without this trivial and vulgar way of coition. It is the foolishest act a wise man commits in all his life; nor is there anything that will more deject his cooled imagination, when he shall consider what an odd and unworthy piece of folly he hath committed. I speak not in prejudice, nor am I averse from that sweet sex, but naturally amorous of all that is beautiful.'

Far from illustrating the solemnity implied in a sacrament, the king of creation in the act of intercourse is one of the most ludicrous creatures imaginable. Consider the opinions that some men have had on the subject. The German philosopher, Schopenhauer, thought that it was 'an act which on sober reflection one recalls with repugnance, and in a more elevated mood even with disgust'. W. T. Stead, a well-known writer of the last generation who had a great interest in the supernatural, expressed the view that the act was 'monstrously indecent', and he could not imagine how two self-respecting people could face each other after having gone through the antics of sexual union together. The English Buddhist adept, Allan Bennett, felt that a god who devised such a bestial and degrading method of propagating the species was a god delighting in loathsomeness and not a god worthy of being worshipped.

Some have held that sex was the primary evil, lying at the very core of nature, and the original sin of mankind. This was another view, and also a religious one. The very source of mortal being was corrupted by the corruption of Adam and Eve. Sex was not part of the divine dispensation but a satanic mystery, a trap set at the boundary of hell for the unwary wayfarer journeying through life. The post-coital melancholy that people experience comes not as a consequence of physical depletion and weariness but from an ingrained sense of guilt. Sex was not God's doing but the Devil's and was under the governance of what St Paul calls 'the Prince of the Power of the Air'. Consequently, and not illogically, sexual desire was thought to be stimulated by wind, an idea that lent itself at times to elaboration with rather crude emphasis. An ancient prohibition against wind-creating foods derived partly from the fact that wind was considered a contributory cause of erection and so aroused sexual desire. Among the ten kinds of wind classified in yogic texts, one called *apana* was thought to be rectumnal and erotic. Sexual union a sacrament! The fuel for the fine flame of love, the misanthropist will point out, is as often as not just flatulence. While the act of love is being passionately conducted in the foreground with words of tender affection, the operating member is being buttressed up in the background by the element of air.

Further, continue the critics, in the physiotaxis or arrangement of bodily parts in the human being, the proximity of the organs of generation and excretion are far from exhibiting the highest wisdom unless indeed this, too, is part of the diabolical design. In some pagan rituals the whole genital and anal area used to be dedicated to the gods of generation in enactments of the most flagitious character, and there is no doubt that erotic forms of worship which treat semen and excremental substances as dedicatory offerings, are amongst the most unpleasant in the whole history of sexual mysticism. In certain cults even today this area serves as the central altar in a form of secret meditation, during which the organs are internally conjoined by a respiratory technique with the cerebral plexus to produce a condition of prolonged orgasm without emission, supposedly akin to a state of mystic trance and union with the Absolute.

Far from exemplifying the divine geometry the genitals have been the cause of man's downfall, and have never ceased to exercise their tyranny over him. Sex holds an eternal fascination for the human race. In quite a literal sense too, for the word 'fascination' comes from the Latin word for the male organ, *fascinum*, and a sexual intention may be discerned in most forms of allurement and glamour. The sex attributes were not part of the original equipment of Adam and Eve. They were not God-given but bestowed by Satan and thus became the instruments of man's undoing and remain an ever-present memento of his fall.

Interestingly enough the phallus was thought, both by primitive and civilised peoples, to have a separate and independent existence, beyond the jurisdiction of the human will. An aboriginal tribe in East Africa believed that the phallus was the abode of a disobedient animal that directed its actions. A tribe of Indians in Brazil thought that a snake dwelt in the penis. And men of more exalted intellect have expressed the same conviction about the 'unruly member' in different terms. 'In man,' writes Plato, 'the nature of the genital organs is disobedient and self-willed, like a creature that is deaf to reason, and it attempts to dominate all because of its frenzied lusts.' In his Epistle to the Romans, St Paul said, 'I see another law in my members warring against the law of my mind'. Schopenhauer felt that 'the genitals are the real focus of the Will and thus opposite to the brain which represents Idea'. And St Augustine came to the conclusion that man could not govern his genitals, and that the 'pudenda' of men and women were so named (from Latin *pudere*, to be ashamed) because 'they expose the shame of men who although able to control all things to their obedience cannot control these parts'.

Medieval tradition regarded the male organs as being within the province of the Devil and there was a popular belief that Satan kept a store of such appurtenances which he dispensed to his followers for distribution to the faithful. One story has it that a young man wished to attend the sabbat and, feeling that he was insufficiently endowed by nature, went to a witch and asked for the loan of one from her store. She told him to climb a tree and help himself from the nest in which they lived and moved about and where she fed them on corn. Rather too ambitiously the youth picked up an outsize specimen but when the witch saw it she told him to put it back. He could take any one he liked, she said, except that one, because that was reserved for the parish priest. A variant of this tale, repeated more than once in medieval writings, also occurs in the *Malleus Maleficarum*, a treatise on witchcraft written in 1486 by two Dominican monks.

But although Satan furnished the sex organs he had nothing to do with the life-bearing effluvium that emanated therefrom, for that was a divine endowment. Satan could not create it and legend tells of the strange expedients he and his minions resorted to in order to obtain the precious seed.

An episode in the *Odyssey* relates how Ulysses, in order to call up the spirit of the dead seer Tiresias for advice, dug a trench and filled it with the blood of slaughtered sheep. The smell of fresh gore attracted the 'strengthless dead' from the depths of Erebus who came crowding around squeaking like bats to partake of the vitalising fluid, so eager were they to regain some semblance of their fleshly vitality. Ulysses had to drive them off by brandishing his sword until Tiresias had come and taken his drink first so that he might have the energy to give Ulysses the counsel he sought.

The mystique of blood is universal, and spirits were often thought to feast on the vapours emanating from shed blood. A corollary of this ancient belief is found in the mystique of seminal essence. Semen has been described as blood filtered through the testes, and according to those versed in such matters, its correct utilisation can call up spirits from the vasty deep as surely as can blood itself. This incredible delusion forms the basis of one of the more disagreeable rites of left-hand occultism, but it is found in folklore as well, and has had a tenacious hold on men's imagination for centuries.

Just as there are supposed to be vampires that suck the blood of human beings, so there are vampires who subsist on the efflux of men. These terrible beings are called succubi. In demonology the ancestress of all the succubi was Lilith, daughter and mistress of Samael, the form in which Satan seduced Eve. She is a creature of wondrous beauty who figures in rabbinical legend as the personification of female lust. She seduced Adam and from the seed of their conjugation produced a brood of vampirish beings whose duty it was to collect the male seed and bring it to Satan who would store it in his repository, much as the modern scientist stores the sperm of bulls.

The succubi drew their substance in three ways. They could do it by materialising and going through actual bodily coition with men, their victims being semi-conscious of their presence at the time and having full enjoyment of the act. Or else they could do it by *congressus subtilis* – by sexual intercourse in a non-corporeal form with the astral body of the sleeping man. Most commonly though, they collected the expended substance of onanism, involuntary emissions, 'wet dreams', homosexuality, and bestiality.

The succubi are sexless but can assume a male or female shape at will. The male was known as an incubus, and it was his business to seduce women and transmit the seed previously taken from the satanic store to impregnate them, concentrating his attention on married women and nuns in order to compound the sin of lust with the broken vows of fidelity and chastity. It was commonly believed that every time the seed was transported to and fro in this manner and exposed to the atmosphere it became suffused with a malignant aura as a result of its contact with the Powers of the Air. In the confessions of medieval witches the sperm of demons with whom they had coitus was almost invariably described as 'cold as ice'.

In the occult tradition the child born out of the duly consecrated womb of a woman united by religious ties to her husband was protected from such demonic contamination, but the offspring created by artificial insemination through the intermediary of an incubus carried the stigma of the elemental and were not truly human. The pure elemental lacks proper corporeality and material composition. It is ethereal in substance although it partakes to some extent of the nature of the element it inhabits. Elementals live in sylvan dells and glades (fairies), inside hills (gnomes and elves), under the earth (cobolds), in the fire (salamanders), in the air (sylphs), in trees (dryads and hamadryads), in pools and rivers (naiads), in islands in the sea (lorelai and sirens), or in the sea itself (nymphs).

Elementals lack a soul and seek to form a liaison with human beings in order to acquire one. They are capable of sexual intercourse and of having children as a result. Folktales of all nations tell of such creatures and their love for mortals. The progeny of such human-elemental unions include legendary super-heroes like Hercules and Achilles, semi-legendary characters like Merlin, and even historical personalities such as Romulus and Remus, founders of Rome, the philosopher Plato, Alexander the Great, and Julius Caesar. Many famous royal and ducal houses of England and France trace their mythical origin to some such amorous encounter between human and elemental. Among them are the Merovingian and Carlovingian kings (the latter including Charlemagne), the Normans and Plantagenets of England, and the Counts of Poitiers and of Luxembourg, to name but a few.

Belief in elementals and the succubi dies hard, and this is strikingly illustrated in a case recorded by J. K. Huysmans (*d.* 1907), French author of *La Bas*, one of the most sacrilegious novels ever to become a classic. Having written his terrible *chef-d'oeuvre* Huysmans fell into a state of profound melancholy and retired for a time to a Trappist monastery to purge his soul after his long travels in what he calls the 'latrines of the supernatural'. And while in his retreat, he had an encounter with such a vampire – a complete facsimile of the entire erotic drama from loveplay to climax. Then at the moment of acute and almost painful ejaculation he awoke and disturbed his astral visitor. Succubi are said to vanish with incredible speed and Huysmans caught a flicker of her as she burst out of sight. The sheet she shared with him was still in disarray and took a moment or two to settle down after she had fled. The fact that Huysmans, an eminently rational man and a greatly respected literary figure of his time, did not attribute this experience to an ordinary erotic dream common to most men shows how deeply the ancient traditions can influence the judgment of a person of high intelligence.

Satan was not alone in setting a high value on the vital product of men, and an almost universal power came to be associated with it. The mystery of its creation within the inmost parts of the male, its lodgement within the sanctuary of the scrotum, and its significance in that it marks the climax of the act of intercourse and is drawn out of the very soul of the male in a spasm that almost seems to shift his personality out of its moorings, was indeed calculated to stun the imagination. The vital fluid became creative in its own right.

In the Bible God gave the mandate to be fruitful and multiply before Eve was created from Adam's rib. Numerous stories in all the mythologies tell how men, demons, and even gods arose from seed fortuitously ejected. In Hebrew writings etheric creatures were said to arise spontaneously from every emission although invisible to the human eye. In Hindu legend there are numerous instances of superhuman heroes and damsels springing up from the expended substance of holy men without the intervention of females. Such emissions wherever they fell, into a canebrake, into a bucket, into a pot, or into the sea resulted in the birth of great rishis, kings, and even deities.

Greek mythology tells how the god Uranus was castrated by his son while he was making love to his wife Ge. From the severed parts replete with the fullness of the creative energy of Uranus there flowed a rich stream of fertilising ichor. It fell from heaven into the raging sea below and from the foaming mass (Greek *aphros*, foam) slowly took shape the most beauteous being that ever was, the goddess Aphrodite, known to the Romans as Venus.

Arabic lore also cites instances of generation without female intermediation, and Chinese folk tradition bears evidence of a similar belief. Paracelsus, counted among the most reputed of medieval physicians and occultists, allegedly had a recipe for making a homunculus or 'little man' by preserving human sperm in a glass phial, fed on a secret pabulum. He did not divulge the full details for fear of the serious consequences that might arise from the abuse of such knowledge.

Besides being spontaneously creative sperm was and still is credited with various supernatural properties and virtues. It has considerable magnetic power, so that those who refrain from sexual activity are believed to be able to draw men and women to themselves through its irresistible attractive force, if they know how. In addition it has the physical property of generating a great thermal current within the human body, as we shall see when we come to consider Tibetan sex mysticism. It has a tremendous psychic and intellectual potential. A sub-sect of the Gnostics, pseudo-Christians who flourished in Egypt and Western Asia during the first four or five centuries of our era, were said to be in the habit of mixing the fluid with the sacramental draught in their religious ceremonies. Compounded in part from the same substance was the *vinum sabati*, the wine drunk at the witches' sabbat, the preparation of which was a great secret and which had the effect of rendering a person's soul immune to the decent life.

There is supposed to be an intimate connection between the 'condition' of the seed and our deeper thoughts. A modern self-styled expert on the subject, Aleister Crowley, probably drawing the logical conclusion from a contemporary school of psychology, held that art, literature, and philosophy were all the outcome of sexual power, and that the whole psychological set-up in man, including the conscious and unconscious, was a radiating miasma from the seminal stream. 'Mind,' he concluded, 'is a disease of semen.'

Sexual energy is linked with the nervous system, hence continence has generally been regarded as obligatory for aspirants to intellectual and spiritual eminence. Those who are devoted to study refrain from sexual activity, and athletes under training submit to a similar privation. Depletion of sexual energy is almost universally believed to devitalise the male and in extreme cases weakens the psyche sufficiently, it is sometimes said, to permit its temporary dislodgement by an alien entity.

In many men a guilt and anxiety complex persists even in a normal male-female relationship. This feeling is widespread and continues despite the assurance of physicians that the human organism benefits from sexual activity and that the lethargy characteristic of the post-coital period is natural, and that in any case there is no depletion that a little diet and deep breathing will not put right.

The facts, according to some occultists, indicate that it is not merely the physical loss that seems to be the disturbing factor. Some vital potency in man is also believed to ebb with each expenditure of the seminal fluid as if his very mana were thereby diminished. The human being is not an organism, they say, that can be considered outside the context of his other, spiritual, self. Semen, like blood, has an occult energy and its expenditure causes a definite erosion in the individual's psyche, and that is not a matter of a little fresh air and a little extra milk and honey.

Where such pathological anxiety is likely to lead we shall see when we deal with the ascetics.

7
Thought-Forms

PSYCHOLOGISTS have, for some time now, been conducting experiments to determine whether an act of will can control the throw of dice. The adept takes it for granted that thought has not only kinetic but creative energy. 'The will of man,' said Paracelsus, 'is a most potent agent. The human spirit is so great that no man can express it. Thought is the only magic.'

All that mankind has achieved is an overflow from thought. Epochal movements are often conjured up out of the will of a single individual. Great revolutions and reigns of terror have been sparked off by solitary thinkers. Thought and emotion are mighty agents of transformation. The dark broodings of a man under great stress can spread gloom about him like a storm-cloud, and raging passions are a furnace that can make the surroundings seethe like a cauldron. Under the influence of very powerful emotions the mind, it is said, can create and project thought-forms that have an independent life of their own. The Arab genius, Avicenna (*d.* 1037), remarked that there exists in the human mind a certain power capable of bringing objects into existence.

Man is a living talisman. His body is surrounded by an aura of subtle vibrations invisible to ordinary sight but perceptible to sensitives, and any deliberate and purposeful action strengthens its power. Such a belief is of long standing. Activation of the physical stirs the superphysical and a movement in consciousness stimulates the superconsciousness. A man's aura can become charged with the intensity of his thoughts, as when he is wrapt in meditation, or deeply immersed in a problem, or filled with fervent devotion, or emotionally excited. At all such times the rate of vibration, as it were, is increased, and the charge of the atmosphere around him stepped up, creating a powerful emanation in his vicinity.

Religious ceremonial and the supernatural are thought to be invisibly linked. Once ritual activity purposively directed is begun the wheel of occult power is set in motion and the impulses thus generated can reach out with great energy towards the higher planes. It has been further claimed that any person who is sufficiently sensitive can feel the vibrations radiating from the vicinity when an occult rite is being performed. The functioning priest with hands raised to bless, the witch doctor pointing a bone, the Druid standing on one leg while uttering a curse, all form the focus through which power is concentrated and projected. Each gesture of the functioning hierophant is supercharged with power.

Any action performed in unison with a larger group, as in the greater religious celebrations, further augments the psychic force. When religious enthusiasm is stirred in the masses just as when political passions are unloosed, the shimmering waves created around the participants can become agitated in tempestuous surges and overwhelm even those not directly concerned with what is being said and done. Like the violence generated during a Nazi political rally, the emotional effects of great revival meetings have been likened to medieval epidemics of demon possession.

Religious feeling, then, is a great source of power. Sexual activity is another. A form of vibratory energy rises spontaneously from such operations just as vapour steams up from a tropical marsh in summer. In particular sexual desire, which often approximates to frenzy, is a radiant energy creating a psychical state akin to inspiration or possession. Many primitive peoples believe that during sexual excitement a man's body becomes the abode of a spirit, and highly sophisticated people too have been aware of the strange and obscene tides that surge into a man's soul and carry him away when he is in the grip of sexual excitement.

The forces generated during the sexual act are said to be of the same order as the religious; both create powerful repercussions in the spiritual world. Posture, purpose, and passion concentrate an energy of great potency. In ordinary intercourse this energy is normally dissipated, but it can be channelled and transmitted.

The position assumed is important. Eve was formed from the front of Adam, and union brings man and woman together again face to face; hence it was generally thought that such a position was the only permissible one for the creative act. There is a kabbalistic tradition that the substance of original sin was not sexual intercourse but sexual aberration. Samael (Satan) seduced Eve in a perverse way and she conveyed this evil knowledge to Adam. All aberrant postures were thus regarded as inspired by the Devil, and the human couple using them – whether they knew it or not, whether they willed it or not – became the medium for the concentration of an evil power.

The fact that a number of postures are possible during intercourse is something that has naturally suggested itself to men and women the world over. Certain cultures have put the art into systematic form and have evolved scores of so-called 'venereal figures', with the mating pair in every possible attitude. Hindu erotic manuals have acquired a certain notoriety for the almost gymnastic contortions suggested by their experts. The people of ancient Mesopotamia and Canaan were also proficient in the finesse of love-making as were the Chinese and Arabs. Through the Arabs the fashion for variety filtered with a great deal of other curious arts into Spain and thence into the rest of Europe. In the 16th century Pietro Aretino (*d.* 1557) put the perverse lore into verse and soon artists were interpreting the verses in paintings. Modern sexologists have given some of these positions their scientific endorsement.

In the occult tradition the postures of union are regarded as something more than a method of enhancing pleasure, providing a variation from the monotony of face to face congress, or a means of subserving some physiological end.

A posture is an arrangement of the human body, and the disposition of one's limbs during the creative act automatically sets in motion the psycho-spiritual stream. Each posture has its occult potency. The Hindu god, Shiva, brought the 8,400,000 living species into existence by merely assuming their imagined forms. He crouched on all fours and projected his nose and an elephant was born; he extended his arms, and behold an eagle! A form is not an unrelated existence or a meaningless arrangement. It is the shape of an energy. Every shape determines the kind of force pattern that emerges from it, and the manner in which it will operate. There is a profound meaning in posture: whether it be one of praying, blessing, cursing, or coition.

A particular arrangement of the limbs is deliberately assumed in a religious rite. The ancients dedicated many of their acts to the gods of generation and fertility and hence their ceremonies were often worked out in phallic symbolism. The Nabateans of ancient Mesopotamia ritually enacted a number of their agricultural rites. Sowing, a natural operation, was accompanied by the natural act of intercourse. The grafting of one plant in a forcible and unnatural manner on to the body of another was correspondingly dramatised in a perverse rite, in order to raise a perverse power and render the graft effective: a young girl specially prepared for the function was made to insert the graft into the tree, and as she bent down to do so a man had unnatural congress with her *a tergo*.

The limbs and organs of man are so arranged that he can by the disposition of his body form a vessel, by gestures articulate his power, and thereby become the vehicle for the operation of a spiritual force. Thus posture facilitates the interpenetration of two worlds. In Tantrik sex mystical rites, the participating agents locked in sexual embrace assume certain fixed symbolic poses and remain thus poised without movement, forming a plastic mould through which occult potencies are drawn down.

Against the background of this belief it becomes easier to understand what a phallic rite can mean to the practitioner. Although the psychologist can explain the entities that are alleged to arise from the energy generated by a sexual rite as subjective creations of a disordered mind, these entities have an objective existence for the magician, and he has evolved various methods by which he can, so he believes, trap their power and use it.

The potencies actualised by the various operations of the sex act differ considerably, and each type is believed to create or draw into its ambit a phantom after its own kind. The solitary act differs from the dual, and the latter from the group orgy. The nature of the act, the kind and number of the participants, their manner of performance, whether natural or unnatural, whether with 'postures' and artificial aids, determine the nature and character of the possessing entity, and the 'colour' of its energy.

Generally speaking the more heinous the sin, by orthodox religious standards, the more powerful and malignant the force created through the intermediary of the offending participants. Adultery, defloration, homosexuality, each cause cross-currents of turbulent energy and charge the atmosphere with envenomed flashes. All are common among adepts, and to gain the special kind of initiation he may need, a man may very well have intercourse with his own grandmother or other partners within the prohibited degrees. These grade off into bizarre unions with animals and, as some believe possible, with elementals and other denizens of the occult deep. The astral ghouls thus created have a mythology of their own. All this is very devious and dangerous territory and the literature virtually inaccessible.

The being that looms over the solitary acts of 'imaginary intercourse' is an evanescent phantom. It is described as a hollow, slimy creature, grey in colour and with a muddy smell, and is dissipated in a few hours unless charged by magical rituals to stay animate, as some sorcerers claim to be able to do with phantoms thus evoked. Atum, an ancient Egyptian god worshipped at Heliopolis, embodies this tradition when he says, 'I held my membrum in my hand. I copulated with my fist. I joined myself in embrace with my shadow.' By this means he created Shu, the atmosphere god, and Tefnut, goddess of moisture.

A similar magical motive may be implied in the sin of Onan mentioned in the Bible. Although the act was one of *coitus interruptus* his sin is traditionally regarded as that of self-abuse. Onan was the son of a woman of Canaan, a country typifying for the Jews all that was reprehensible and devilish in religion, with its ritual oblations of the human seed to demons and the embracings of shadows conjured up, for the boon of fertility and the furtherance of diabolism. Onan was not otherwise punished for a sin that is practically universal among adolescents, and that often survives maturity and sometimes even marriage.

When two people get together for sexual purposes the shape, colour, and life-expectancy of the 'shadows' that emerge from their union is determined by what they do, their sex, and their methods of performance. The kabbalistic tradition of medieval Jewry expressed this idea by describing what happens in the invisible world when a man and woman married in a religious ceremony come together in normal intercourse. As they unite two diaphanous forms assemble over their heads in the shape of whirling wheels and fuse together, assuming slowly the outline of a funnel in the increasing passion of their union. If the male sperm is destined to unite with the egg within the womb a spiritual eidolon is drawn into the funnel from the realm of the 'real'. It is actualised by their sanctified union out of the treasury of souls in heaven that await embodiment. This astral being hovers quiescently over the woman and she remains thus overshadowed until the time of quickening when it enters her body. Thus is a divine soul incarnated in a human frame.

A group of three or more persons uniting together also create their own occult atmosphere, and there is a difference between groups indulging in a debauch and those performing a religious rite in which sexuality is present. Within the first category are to be placed the revels of ancient Rome, which were chiefly drinking bouts interspersed with other sensual pleasures. These may be regarded rather as cathartic in character, a means of letting off steam. The sexual element here was not highlighted by any religious emotion.

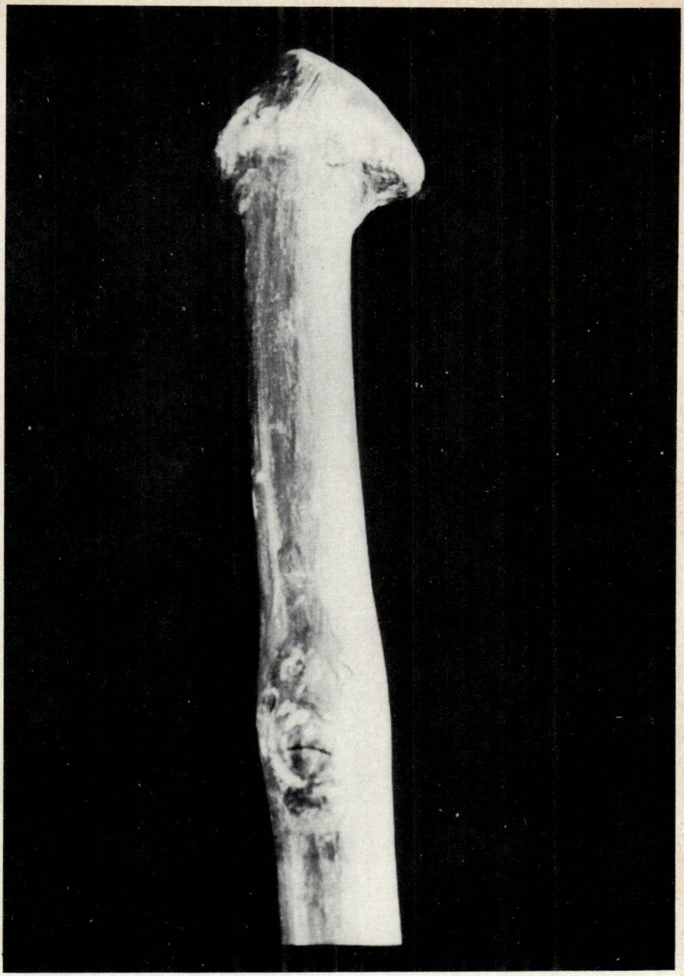

1. Phallic-headed broomstick from the Witches' Mill Museum, Isle of Man.

2. Carvings on roof-supports of Nepal temples dedicated to the Hindu god, Shiva — The Creator, The Preserver, The Destroyer, The creative side of the god's nature being all important, various methods of performing the sex act are depicted.

3. The concept of duality — the hermaphrodite, as represented in many early alchemical works.

4. *The Temptation of St Anthony* by Patinir who depicts the saint resisting the allure of beautiful succubi.

5. In India a widow was considered essential company for her husband in the afterworld and might be buried alive or burnt alive with her husband's body.

At puberty, thought to be a form of initiation into adulthood, the boys of primitive societies are circumcised.

6. *Below*. Boys in Azande join in a ceremonial dance.

7. *Right*. Young aborigines prepare themselves for the operation.

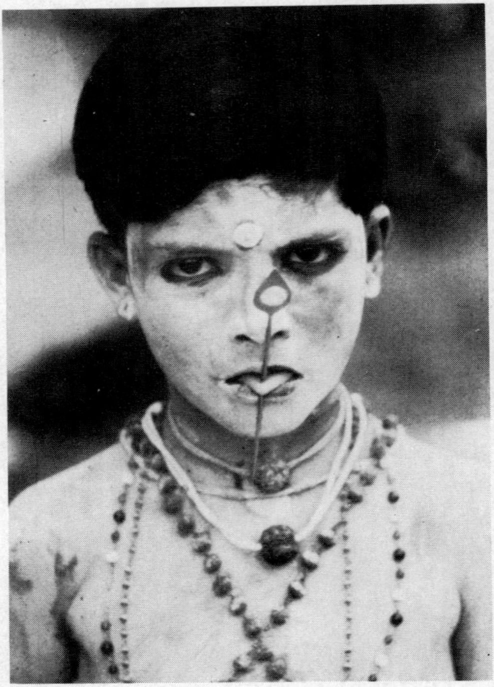

8. A 'trainee' Ascetic in India, with a pin through his tongue.

But there is another kind of orgy in which the erotic element is linked with the religious, and here the 'magnetic' field around the participants has the force of a psychic storm. The exaltation that inspired the celebrants of these ancient cults was in the nature of a divine experience, and a far cry from the debauch of the besotted Roman with naked catamites in attendance and a slave to tickle his throat with a feather so that he might regurgitate what he had eaten and drunk and start all over again.

In the cultic rites of ancient Syria and Phrygia a mystery was enacted by the participants who were charged initially with a high degree of religious fervour. This type of orgy was a supernatural occasion and in it sex was used as a means to an end in order to heighten a religious mystery. The maenads ('raving' women) who participated with hair streaming, mouth flecked with foam and eyes glazed, were in the mood of 'enthusiasm'. In the Greek meaning of the term the word signified 'god-possessed', and they showed symptoms allied to madness as they danced with hips convulsed with orgasmic frenzy and uttered their shrill ululations that made the hills and forests re-echo and sent the frightened wolf back to its lair.

Accounts of medieval sabbats similarly suggest a surrender by 'enthusiastic' groups of their personalities to satanic powers which were actually the rising tides from within themselves that flooded the being and overwhelmed them, inducing a state of trance and dissociation. There were a number of understanding witnesses to these phenomena who attributed the confession of witches to dementia and delusion or plain erotic hallucination, allied to the wish-dreams of the nymphomaniac for the ravishing satyr. But the Church authorities were not unaware of the deep-seated inheritance from the pagan past in which nature spirits, many of a priapic character, were worshipped as gods and were believed to take possession of their devotees. The true sabbat they regarded as an orgy with a religious intent, where allegiance to Satan was betokened by trampling on the Cross, a new baptism of blood, and a pact with the Devil sealed with a kiss on the Devil's behind.

Wherever spiritual frenzy is aroused in conjunction with sexual activity an intense power is believed to emanate from the celebrants and a tremendous dynamism is thought to surcharge the atmosphere, providing a medium for the spirits of the underworld who, fortified by the pabulum, displace the individual personalities and 'possess' the participants thus inducing their 'enthusiasm'. Black magical ceremonies of more recent times, described with great realism in novels by modern occultists, show how a delirium of this kind can be induced among a large group of celebrants taking part in a ceremony of total consecration to the powers of darkness. Drawn into the vortex swirling up from the generated impulses of the embracing bodies are the invisible entities of the nether regions, like so many gruesome slugs, who seek to displace the souls of the congregation and possess them as long as the mania lasts.

The psyche may be similarly beset by certain kinds of music, which was an invariable accompaniment to the revels. There were trumpet calls and drum-beats to stimulate the nerves and induce uncontrollable reflexes in the brain, lungs, and liver. The zitherist could pluck the heart-strings as easily as the strings of his instrument. Harsh animal rhythms could make a direct appeal to the sexual instinct. Hindu manuals say it is possible by means of certain sounds to induce an orgasm in others. To use the modern idiom, music can reduce its fans to a 'jerk', a word that originally signified a person whose brain was addled and rendered idiotic by self-abuse. The associated word 'jazz' is also suggestive of sexuality. From early times drums were regarded as the abode of devils and in some places were placated with blood offerings. Similarly, wind instruments were thought to arouse the imps of lust. 'Whoever plays the flute,' said St Chrysostom, 'summons the demons.'

There are no high priests in obsessive music because its purveyors are equally victims with their votaries. Like a magical ceremony the musical feast can be a sabbatic rite, and like the orgy can induce spasms, convulsive fits, and even a state bordering on possession.

It has been suggested that certain kinds of spiritualist mediums may also be exposed to psychic assaults during trance, and the fact of 'possession' by an alien entity seems to be fairly generally accepted. The energy for various phenomena including kinetic effects is sometimes provided by those present at a séance, for mediums do occasionally draw from the sitters. The atmosphere in such cases is charged with tension and the sitters are seriously affected and complain of feeling exhausted and ill. But usually the medium herself is the source of the supply needed. Psychical research has established that an 'invisible fluid' emanates from the medium during trance. According to some investigators mediums have been known to shrink and lose weight when a spirit materialises, as if providing some actual substance from themselves for the manifesting form. In materialisations, ectoplasm may issue from the genitals of a female medium, and when the phenomenon is one of great clarity and strength, it has been accompanied in some cases by an orgasm. In the long run such inroads on the nervous system can be devitalising and injurious, and mediums, like musicians, have sometimes felt a craving for stimulants and drugs, as if they needed to restore the balance of the vital power lost in this manner.

8

The Puritan

SENSUALITY involves a loss and wantonness is a form of squandering. Rightly therefore, according to the experts, are such things regarded as 'dissipation'. Sexual activity is the most insidious form of dissipation and the most pervasive, appearing in various guises and causing a tear in the psychical vesture of man, through which valuable energy is needlessly dissipated.

Sexual fulfilment may be good psychology but is poor psychism, for such involvement if carried to excess can be wasteful and pernicious. The subject is very extensive and takes one into many hidden byways of the occult. In certain Eastern systems its study belongs to a metaphysical school of great refinement touching on the doctrine of Nothingness and other privatives, whose practice requires the cultivation of the negative virtues like silence, solitude, and inaction. First the superfluous and then all but the absolutely essential activities are renounced one by one in a kind of progressive disengagement, on the principle that whatever is not conducive to the end in view, is deleterious.

In the western world, too, there have been a number

of comparatively moderate exponents of this view, abstinent by constitution or conviction, who to a greater or lesser degree renounce the pleasures of the table and the bed, and are generally wary of all that pleases the eye, the ear, the palate, the nose and the flesh, and even the intellect. Such were the Puritans, stern people who frowned on secular enjoyments, beautiful clothes and other luxuries, and would, if they could, even restrain laughter. They have come in for considerable vilification as representing all the narrow-mindedness and impure suspicion of the hidden pervert. Their critics denounce them as the worst elements in the Protestant tradition and exult in the final end of their reign. Killjoys and hypocrites, they are well out of the mainstream of Christian life.

It is perhaps an error to malign Puritanism as a Protestant disease as though the rest of the Christian world knew nothing about it – starting from the early Church Fathers, Puritans have been ubiquitous in Christianity – or to speak of it as something specifically Christian, when vast areas of Judaism, Buddhism, Hinduism, and Islam are nothing if not puritanical.

The Puritan was firm in his conviction that he knew what he was talking about. He often saw with Freudian genius the omnipresence of sex, and with crystal clarity the insidious ramifications of sensuality let loose. His extreme suspicion of sex gave him a profound and accurate insight into the pitfalls of amoral freedom, and many people feel that the Puritan had much to say that is still worth listening to, even if his philosophy is underlined in part with heavy emphasis.

Sex is the Puritan's bugbear. All forms of 'release',

he feels, weaken the spirit, and in particular once the floodgates of sex are opened the whole spiritual life can soon be inundated and submerged. Comparing sex to a hunger that must be appeased is a subterfuge of Satan, for countless men and women have done without it. Sex is meant only for procreation, as God has ordained. Used for pleasure it is a form of indulgence foredoomed for dedication to the Evil One.

Zinzendorf, 18th-century reformer of a puritanical sect, taught that there should be no more enjoyment of sex in marriage than of the wine in the sacrament. Love should be kept strictly in check, for marriage did not free a man from the restraints of religious discipline. He had no licence to indulge in any form of sexual activity he pleased whenever he pleased. Jeremy Taylor (*d.* 1667), famous English divine, expressed a curious but long-standing belief that an uxorious husband – one who loved his marriage partner too much – was in danger of an adulterous relationship with her. Just as a mother through over-affection for her child can be guilty of the sin of selfishness, for that is what such excess of love amounts to, so can an infatuated husband be guilty of adultery with his own wife.

There were certain sects of Puritans who used to perform their conjugal duties at dead of night, with the wife fully clothed from neck to ankle in a special heavy gown, the *chemise cagoule*, with only a small rent in the appropriate place. No other touching was permitted, and the act was performed face to face, in complete silence, without preparatory love-play or love-talk. Thus carnality was reduced to a minimum.

To the Puritan pleasure was a snare and sensuality

a sin, and he encouraged the more austere activities of life in order to forestall the devil by reducing the sphere of his operations. He condemned gossip, secular music, theatres, all forms of entertainment, on the principle that 'acts not done for the sake of God are wasted acts'. Profanity was forbidden because it was pagan (it belonged to the ancient seasonal rites), it was sexual (as witness many swear-words), it was sacrilegious (since it often invoked God's name), and above all it was a form of 'relief'. Restraint in self-expression was a wholesome discipline and a means of building up greater reserves of spiritual strength.

The Puritan spoke of joy, by which he meant the inner joy of the Lord, and not the frivolity of laughter, for that implied acquiescence in an ungodly world. Laughter was essentially sexual and vulgar, belonging to the unregenerate multitude. The Greeks applied the epithet *philommeides*, 'laughter-loving', to the meretricious Venus, whose other nickname was Pandemos – belonging to the whole mob, the vulgar. 'Before you drink from a stream,' the Puritan reminds us, 'remember the source.' Greek comedy, the forerunner of European comedy, originated from the rustic horseplay that accompanied the early harvest festivals. The actors carried out in procession wooden penises painted red, recited fescennine poems, sang pornographic songs, and bandied about obscenities, all of which was interspersed with loud noises made by the expulsion of air from a bladder held under the arm and squeezed, suggestive of another cruder sound. Comedy in the Puritan view always retained the marks of its ancient ancestry and belonged to the belly and sex organs. Take away the dirty joke and sexual situation from most comedy and little else remains.

The Puritan regarded the body as an inflammable medium, and all preoccupation with it as likely to jeopardise the soul. Excessive concern for one's health and physical welfare could lead one astray whereas physical disabilities might sometimes be blessings in disguise. He would further add that personal hygiene (named after a pagan goddess) has emancipated woman from the odour of her sex, and since modesty arises from a woman's awareness of her own odour, bathing can become sinful if it enables a woman to parade her sex without fear of being offensive.

Besides, the flesh was imbued with evil and the whole body was an area of voluptuousness inviting stimulation that had to be resisted. Voltaire, in his *Philosophical Dictionary* observes that the love life of man has been enormously increased by the attainment of a higher standard of cleanliness because his whole skin has become more responsive to the sense of touch. Therefore even cleanliness could be overdone. Then, bathing meant taking off one's clothes and nudity to the Puritan was anathema. Nakedness was an invitation to interference and sexual experience. Apart from all this the great danger of being physically washed and clean is that one can then be easily deluded into believing that one is also spiritually pure, or that spiritual purity is of no consequence.

Severe as this outlook may have been it was only one facet of a many-sided philosophy connected with sex and the supernatural, that found its most extended fulfilment in a way of life in which sex was not only suppressed but almost extirpated. The Puritan stood on the brink of it but did not venture in the noisome depths. That was left to the ascetic.

9
Asceticism

THE term asceticism, which means abstinence from material satisfactions and the renunciation of worldly pleasures, comes from the Greek *askesis*, a word originally used for the stringent discipline that athletes underwent during the period of their training.

Asceticism has a universal prevalence and an old history. Ancient Egyptian hierophants in the wilderness of Thebes, medieval Irish monks on windswept rocky islets, aborigines in the Australian bush, Tibetan lamas in icy Himalayan caves, Muslim sufis in the burning desert, Siberian shamans in the barren steppe, were all dedicated to a life of austerity in one form or another.

The best known among the Christian ascetics were those who lived in the Thebaid in Egypt and in the Syrian desert between the third and fifth centuries. They lived far from the usual haunts of men, alone and in silence, fasted for long periods or subsisted on a meagre diet of coarse food unappetisingly prepared; beat themselves with knotted cords and nettles, endured without complaint the scorching heat of the summer and the intense cold of winter. Some burdened their bodies with iron chains, others never lay down to sleep, others stood on one leg for weeks at a time.

Perhaps the most celebrated of these 'athletes of God', as they were called, was Simon of Antioch (*d.* 459) known as the Stylite – the 'pillar' man – a hermit who lived on top of a high column and whose fame spread throughout the Middle East so that people came from far-off countries to see him. Another well-known ascetic was Mary the Egyptian (*d.* 400), a woman of great beauty once given over to a life of pleasure who was suddenly converted, and retired to the desert. Seventeen years later she was described as having a vaguely human shape, a body blackened by exposure to the sun, and a skin tough and thick from being battered by the fierce desert winds.

The majority of these recluses lived in squalor, none ever bathed, few even washed. This supreme disregard for personal appearance and personal cleanliness is a characteristic trait of the ascetic, and in the eyes of the pious has for long been lauded as a sign of sanctity. There have been Christian saints who were proud of never having wetted their fingers, and few even among the higher prelates of the Church changed their undergarments at hygienic intervals. When Thomas à Becket lay on his bier in Canterbury Cathedral and the vermin started crawling out of his cooling body the people, who already regarded him as a saint, wept at this further proof of his holiness.

In our present age when baths are part of the equipment of most homes and the means of having baths are accessible to all, it is easily forgotten how rarely people in times past bathed their bodies. Cleanliness was a luxury and had nothing to do even remotely with godliness, and the few who could afford the luxury were not greatly concerned about personal hygiene. What is more, there was a belief common to a number of religious communities that bodily dirt had a strong magical aura and that washing the body washed off the magic as well; also, that excessive concern for bodily purity, where it did not imply a predilection for sensual delights and sexual indulgence, betokened a guilty consciousness of sin. The remark of the French writer Anatole France (*d.* 1924) that 'Christianity killed the bath' was at least partly true for the Church, if it recommended bathing at all, imposed it in the form of a cold bath, as a penance.

Christianity grew up in Rome and the reputation of the baths of the imperial city may have contributed to no small extent to the suspicion that the Church developed for all forms of secular ablution. The fashion for hot baths had been introduced from Sybaris, a city that stood in the classical world for moral decadence and luxury at its most depraved. So dissolute were the practices that went on in the bathing houses in Rome that even the pagan authorities spoke of them as dens of vice. The worship of certain obscene gods dedicated to the bath included prostitution and all kinds of sexual deviation. The saint who renounced the world and renounced sex, frequently renounced the bath as well.

Asceticism for all its distortions is part of the religious inheritance of humanity in every clime, and although some ascetics may be dismissed as frustrated lovers, masochists, anti-social cranks, or simply psychopaths, a few have been moved by somewhat better motives, however far they may have carried their practices. Men have renounced self-indulgence and pleasure because they deemed it sinful, or because it is degrading, because it is a concession to weakness, because it is transient and no permanent benefit ensues from its pursuit. Renunciation purges the soul of its impurities and strengthens the spirit, and for that reason must be sought and endured.

Countless men born to luxury and high estate have renounced their wealth and privileges to embrace the harsh life of the ascetic. The cruel edge of the anchorite's discipline seems to provide the searing experience their souls crave. Imperceptibly they acquire at the same time the inner power that comes from a disciplined will.

This then is another reason behind renunciation. A supernatural one. Give up and you get back a hundredfold. And giving up implies among other things the surrender of the sensual appetites to the will. The reward of renunciation is peace of soul and a place in paradise, but it has its rewards here too. In the mundane sphere psychology recognises the fact that the sexual instinct or libido when conserved can be sublimated in science, politics, literature, and religion. The French writer, Gustave Flaubert, advised young artists to lead a life of repression so as to intensify their creative impulse. Controlled sexual energy enhances personal magnetism; intensifies the dynamism of the body; heightens the spiritual faculties. Having mastered the self a man can easily master others. From there on he can rise to control the elemental forces and the forces of nature.

By means of austerities the yogi seeks *siddhis* or supranormal powers which will give him command over man, nature, and the supernatural. In Hindu mythology the rishis of ancient renown knew the value of self-denial and were able to work up so much power as a result of their austerities that they sent waves of disturbance through the cosmos and caused consternation in heaven. The gods had one infallible remedy for this dangerous state of things. They would hurriedly send down to earth the most voluptuous of their heavenly nymphs who would parade in transparent robes before the emaciated celibate. The sight of her would break the continuity of his concentration and more often than not he would be unable to resist her attractions. The result of his downfall would be the restoration of order in the universe.

In a normal man asceticism can lead to a growing obsession with libidinous thoughts. The desires provoked by long sexual repression can grow into a raging turbulence in the mind. St Jerome (*d.* 420) tells of the fierce assaults made upon him by his own desires. 'Often while I was living in the desert amid scorpions and wild beasts, I used to fancy myself amid the pleasures of Rome, among bevies of young women. My skin was dry and my frame gaunt from fasting and penance, my body was that of a corpse, yet my mind was aflame with the cravings of desire, and the fire of lust burned in my flesh.'

In the accounts of other religious mystics these erotic visions were frequently accompanied by other varieties of sensual allure such as provocative perfumes and seductive voices. Often female forms actually became visible. The psychologist would explain such phenomena as hallucinations engendered by repression, but to the person concerned they have a vivid reality, and to the occultist may represent a genuine materialisation. With St Anthony, another recluse who lived alone, the assaults took the form of phallic demons and obscene phantoms who haunted his imagination, invaded his dreams, and finally actualised before him, tantalising him with their suggestions. The 'temptations' that assailed him could very well have been, according to occult theory, thought-forms created by suppressed desire and having a very real existence.

What comes to the religious ascetic unbidden, the sorcerer conjures up by a deliberate magical process. His routine follows the same pattern as the anchorite's but he hastens his objective by a tortuous provocation of sexual desire. The power thus generated by abstinence may either be turned back upon himself to recharge his own psychic batteries, or forged into a psychic missile and projected outwards towards its goal. Visualisation is the key to the occult, and a powerful thought dynamised by the imagination is one of the secret weapons of the magician. He creates a thought-form, a phantom entity that can be set to work, like a zombie of the etheric. It can be made to enter the astral background of a person's dreams, or to haunt his waking moments by voicing suggestions to him, compel him to commit any act at its prompting, and even drive him to suicide. All such servitors of the sorcerer are projected creations of his own thoughts, and the most vicious are those that emerge during a phase of aroused desire, deliberately augmented by a method of repeated stimulation continuously suppressed.

The technique of adding sexual refinements to passive asceticism and teasing one's self-control to near bursting point in order to heighten the tensions of power was known to a number of communities with a sophisticated sex-magical tradition. The Tantriks of India have a form of private worship, in association with women, when such power is cumulatively built up. The rite, preceded by a period of celibacy, is accompanied by the drinking of aphrodisiacs, and may last for hours, sometimes for days, while the practitioner raises the energy thus enormously empowered by restraint, from the physical to the psychical plane, in this case in order to experience a state of spiritual enlightenment.

The Arab world knew something similar in the Bedouin cult of the Beni Udhra, which also employed the same technique of desire deliberately aroused and deliberately denied satisfaction. Sexual love being akin to spiritual love, the arousal of the sexual instinct creates, it is thought, a corresponding excitement of the spiritual faculties. Udhrism was practiced by men and women in closest intimacy short of fulfilment, which according to different authorities meant variously: short of penetration, short of movement after penetration, and above all short of climax. With the male the prolongation of the act and the control of emission was assisted by what was called *imsak*, or 'retention', which required special preparatory training. Both partners might be transported in waves of bliss during the brink-of-climax state, which was directed towards spiritual ends, but also, during a period of temporary cessation, to the more practical purposes of inspiring literary creativity. The cult which was extolled by certain Arab poets spread from Baghdad to Spain and beyond, and influenced the Courts of Love and the Provençal poets who, like their Arab counterparts, seem to have drawn inspiration from the erethitic mood for the writing of erotic verse and mystical poetry.

In so far as sex fulfilment allays internal tension it fulfils a biological need, but while doing so it abrades the discontent that provides the frictions so necessary for sparking the higher facilities. If love unfulfilled provokes poetry, then at a higher remove it may induce a mystical rapture. The ecstatic passages in the writings of mystics are often near enough to eroticism to arouse the interest of the psychopathologists, although it would perhaps be only fair to attribute such mystical transports to the inadequacies of language in expressing the full intensity of religious devotion, and not always to regard them as the outpourings of a suppressed libido.

Several cults have been acquainted with the rationale of restraint, and employed techniques of self-control in varying degrees. How intimations of this practice, much watered down, reached America is not known, but it achieved a certain notoriety as part of the mystical system of John Humphrey Noyes (*d.* 1886) who founded a community in Oneida Creek, New York State, in the middle of the last century. The Biblical injunction to love one another Noyes interpreted as being impeded in its fullest operation by the monogamous Christian marriage. Men and women must literally love as many of the opposite sex as possible, and not claim exclusive possession of their spouses. Union was permitted and encouraged with anyone of the opposite sex. Young boys were introduced into the mysteries of sex by older women, and young girls by older men. Noyes bowed to public opinion and abandoned the practice of 'complex marriage' as it was called, but his system of 'male continence', later known as *coitus reservatus*, was taken up outside his community by enthusiastic converts. In this system a woman's needs were gratified and yet the man's energy was conserved by his withholding orgasm, and both were provided with a spiritual experience. The technique was championed and further elaborated by Mrs Alice Bunker Stockham in her book *Karezza*, published in 1896. Neither man nor woman was to strive for orgasm, unless of course children were the aim. They both reached the high-point of tension and when the end was imminent they just lay perfectly still until the moment passed, and then carried on until the next moment of pre-climax. Although the fullest point was never attained, the graph of ecstasy could be marked by a wavy line that never reached the peak but remained high above the normal and maintained its gentle rise and fall over a period of one or two hours, both partners remaining throughout in a condition of tumescence and heightened intensity.

In time 'karezza' was believed to bestow extraordinary physical, mental, and spiritual blessings. An increased sexual potency and greater youthfulness were the immediate consequences of continued practice in the art; a sense of lightness was communicated to the body and also a sense of levitation, giving one the feeling of hovering in the air. The mental benefits were a more perceptive consciousness and an awareness of the glowing beauty of natural phenomena. Finally there was the reward of mystical experience, a feeling of supreme exaltation and ecstasy, with the promise of reaching in time the greatest heights in the spiritual planes.

The excruciating self-control demanded by these cults, whether practiced in Arabia, India or elsewhere, was obviously beyond the capacity of more than a few, as not everyone had the will-power to deny himself the culminating pleasure. So long as the operative organ was present sexual restraint could not always be ensured. As a result of this, some sects came into being who permanently bound the offending member until it dried up and atrophied, or took the drastic step of castration.

The history of castrant sects goes back to very early times. It reached its height in rites connected with the worship of the great mother goddess in ancient Syria during which young celebrants, duly fortified by drugs and roused to religious frenzy stepped forth to the altar and in the presence of all cut off their organs and flung them at the foot of the idol.

Whether a mystical experience was always sought as a result of this sacrifice is not clear, but it does seem to have been the aim of the best known of the modern castrant cults called the Skoptsi, or 'eunuchs', a mystical Russian sect which first came into prominence in the middle of the 18th century but which was said to have been in existence for at least three centuries before that. The Skoptsi regarded sexual activity as physically revolting and spiritually devitalising and, on joining, the new member refrained from all sexual intercourse. If he wished to rise in the hierarchy he had to submit to the ceremony of the First Seal, castration, which was performed by cutting off the testicles with a curved knife or burning them with a red-hot iron. The breasts of women were treated in the same manner. Skoptsi adepts claimed to be in possession of a deep secret which was revealed only to those who took the final step and accepted the Second Seal, removal of the penis, since its presence was an impediment to the understanding of the secret. It was a way to the acquisition of great power over man and nature, and gave one supernatural enlightenment. Before the Russian Revolution of 1917 the sect numbered 100,000 persons of both sexes and included members of the aristocracy, high government officials, civil servants, priests, merchants, soldiers, and peasants.

All the deviant practices dealt with so far still proceed on the basis of sex as part of our materiality, and its entanglement with matter. What then is it like to experience sex almost freed from the fleshly vehicle? That is the knowledge sought by a still more curious group of mystics who went in for a kind of death-point sexuality, an extremely dangerous technique of near-suicide linked with exhaustive orgasm, which conjured up a current of such searing power that a whole world of new potentialities was put within their grasp.

A form of death-approximation was sometimes practised in select bawdy houses in Europe by strangulation to the point of unconsciousness to induce satyriasis, but after a notorious case that ended in fatality the risks were not considered worth the money paid to the madames by the patrons who demanded the service. But a near-death rite of sex mysticism was evolved as a cold-blooded device to experience a kind of spiritual lucidity greatly sought after by aspirants to the rarefied heights.

Exhaustion as a method of intensity is among the most secret of secret teachings. In this the ascetic reaches an ecstatic state by privation, attenuating the needs of his body till he barely lives. Exhaustion techniques actively tempt death itself. The body is the victim of the merciless rite. Brother Ass, as St Francis called the physical frame, must be driven to an extremity of fatigue. The average man is a compassionate rider and gives up at the first protesting whinny of his mount. But the body must be goaded till the very last bit of energy seems to be spent. Athletes who keep going when beyond the initial phase of weariness know of a second wind, a sudden spurt of energy that gives them the strength to go yet further than they thought possible. Exhaustion techniques know of a third and fourth and fifth wind. The body at these later stages is no longer under the control of the conscious mind and the practitioner is in a state of almost somnolent existence. At a predetermined point in this semicomatose state, when it seems impossible to do any more, the flame of sex is lit. Exhaustion is piled on exhaustion till the whole bodily apparatus functions like a dumb automaton. The soul's interior is apparently then lit up with a fierce flame that sends its radiance through the core of one's being. Quite obviously exhaustion methods are practicable only for the most resolute-willed, since the average man would be fast asleep long before he even got his second wind. But it is a form of mysticism connected with the journey into the interior planes while in trance, and is used by magicians both black and white, the latter dropping the sexual element from the routine.

The last item in this catalogue of morbid mysticism concerns sex in actual contact with death itself. Buried deep in the human unconscious is a dim awareness of the near-identity of the life-principle, with the power that can extinguish it. Consciously, coition is found in frequent association with violence, pain, and death; orgasm itself where the ego seems to dissolve, being a form of dying. The psychologists say Eros and Thanatos are next of kin. The Arabs say love and death abide in the same tent.

There are many terrible forms of mysticism that are as near to charnel-house sexuality as we shall ever get. The most sinister adepts are found in the East, and it need hardly be said that those who follow the orthodox Eastern religions regard their pursuits as a heinous travesty of their faith.

The dead are everywhere regarded as very potent 'magic'. This age-old belief is not confined to the oriental systems. Corpse-magic, the hand-of-glory, skull and skeleton lore, graveyard superstitions, belief in the hangman's powers and in the magic-working potency of execution-emissions and gibbet-flesh, and all the manifold lore of the gallows, show that it was very much alive in Western tradition as well.

The Eastern necromancer's art, of which not much

need be said here, acquaints him with the old numinous terrors of death, and involves the conjuration of demonic hags (*dakinis*) from the primeval abyss by drawing mystical diagrams (*mandalas*) in the air symbolising their generative organs, while intoning weird syllables that seem to be relics of some lost language. The rites are performed at night, usually in cemeteries and cremation grounds, the physical energy for the apparitions being raised by contact and congress with cadavers animated by magical rites. Frightful beings from the nether regions crowd around, and the initiation given by the *dakinis* is full of psychological horrors that surpass belief. Terror controlled and revulsion overcome is the secret of success in this line of mysticism, which has driven more than one practitioner to madness and sometimes death.

10

A Brief History

THE origin of the oriental systems of sexual magic as found in China, India and Tibet has not been clearly established. Much of the esoteric mysticism of these countries is similar and attempts have been made to trace it to a common source.

A likely diffusion area is a semi-legendary place somewhere in Central Asia and located between Afghanistan and the Gobi Desert, known as Shambhala. Precisely where it was situated and how long its influence lasted is not known, but a hoary tradition has been claimed for it taking it back to remote antiquity. In historical times, one centre of the Shambhala tradition appears to have been known as Urgyan, where practical systems both of phallic sorcery and white magic were taught in secret conclaves. These doctrines spread over a wide area and profoundly influenced the religions of the adjacent countries. Madame Blavatsky, Aleister Crowley, G. I. Gurdjieff, all great travellers and all founders of esoteric schools, have each in their own way made their contribution to the myth of the Eastern, Central Asian and Himalayan adept.

We cannot tell when the stream of occult knowledge first entered China. Masters of Chinese alchemy and sexual mysticism claim to 'honour and practice the words of Huang-Lao', a composite title made up of the names of two different people, and later applied to a single deity. The first name belongs to Huang Ti, the mythical Yellow Emperor of China who lived in 2600 BC, which places him ten centuries before the time traditionally ascribed to Moses. A number of miraculous legends have clung to Huang Ti's name. He was conceived when a flash of lightning caused his mother to become pregnant; he emerged into the world after a gestation of twenty-five months and could speak from birth. He was the author of works on astrology, alchemy and breathing, all long lost, although his teachings were handed down by word of mouth from generation to generation. He it was who first understood the mysteries of absorbing the vital energies of women during congress, and it was said that he was able to have intercourse with 1,200 concubines one after the other without it doing him any harm.

The 'Lao' in the honoured name of Huang-Lao refers to Lao Tzu (d. 520 BC) one of the world's greatest sages, and author of *Tao Te Ching*, a slender classic full of sublime wisdom. The philosophical school founded by Lao Tzu is called Taoism, the doctrine of the 'Way' – although older than Lao Tzu – and after his death he was revered by his people as one of the great teachers of mankind. Strange to say, within three centuries he became known as the father of Chinese occultism and sex practices based on methods of internal alchemy. Perhaps a few stray words in his masterpiece could with some difficulty be strained to reveal a sexual significance, but how the name of this venerable man otherwise came to be associated with the lurid side of Taoism is hard to understand.

The goal of many forms of Chinese esoteric discipline was to prolong life and acquire a sort of earthly immortality. Man's physical frame as normally constituted, however, can stand only so much stress, and for the average man the rigours of some of the ancient methods for achieving these desired ends were not always easy to bear.

Great importance was laid on *tso-wang*, an early system of physical culture, for gaining control over the bodily functions. The regime also included a diet which forbade meat, wine, and five kinds of grain. What these grains actually were is never consistently stated, but they were thought to create evil vapours and fetid emanations which inhibited the circulation of the vital breath and were inimical to health and longevity.

Since not everyone was capable of enduring the gruelling regimen, short cuts were provided in the shape of pills and elixirs, and as a result of generations of theorising about such remedies a form of alchemy was evolved and various recondite recipes formulated. In spite of the prospects of immortality held out by the alchemists to those who swallowed their nostrums, the clients lost their youthfulness and strength like other mortals, became old, grey, and died. The sages then declared that the right ingredients were unobtainable in China and spoke of certain elysian fields far out to sea where they were to be sought. Chinese emperors equipped costly expeditions to search for these islands. Kings, princes, and nobles swallowed enormous quantities of boluses compounded from these new ingredients by court alchemists and drank rejuvenative liquids from life-endowing cups of jade. All in vain: they died in due time and were numbered among their ancestors.

Yet another branch of alchemy dealt with breath (*ch'i*), which had to be inhaled by a process of 'embryonic respiration', such as is natural to a child within the womb, then held internally and purified. From this purified breath one extracted all the nourishment one needed, and then sent the vitalised breath on a circuit through the body to invigorate each part. The chief stations of this journey were known as the Fields of Cinnabar, situated in the heart, the chest, and the abdomen. It was believed that a single lungful of air contained enough energy for the needs of an individual's lifetime. One inhalation sufficed, and it was unnecessary to waste one's strength in breathing in and out so many times a minute. The adept who could hold his breath for three days and extract all the nourishment from just that one inhalation in this manner, could live forever.

Although no one was ever able to endure the strain of such a heroic retention, the practice of alchemy, once it began to be 'internalised', so to speak, produced a score of techniques concerned with breath and the various organs of the body brought into contact with it, as part of a training scheme for obtaining supernatural powers. In its magical phases the potentialising of the breath was especially connected with the sexual apparatus, and breath (*ch'i*) and semen (*ching*) became the two basic principles in this system. Internal alchemy became a method of transmuting the inner man by a process involving these two factors.

But what was the inner man? Well, he had to be created. Just as a child is created from the male seed in man being projected outwards into a woman's womb, so man's internal 'embryo' must be created from the male principle being directed inwards to unite with the female principle within himself. To understand this we must briefly consider a basic concept of Chinese mysticism.

Taoism teaches that the great unitive principle of the universe is revealed in two forms of energy known as yang and yin, which are immanent in all things, so that each thing as we experience it partakes of the nature of these two forces to a greater or lesser degree. In general yang is said to be active, masculine, positive, light; and the yin passive, feminine, negative, dark.

In the human species the male is yang and the female yin. But there is also a yang-yin pattern within each individual. Thus a man is yang, having a woman as his yin; but within himself his head is yang and his heart yin, and several other dualities besides these exist within each person. Such variations in gender provide the opposite stresses required to give things identity, vitality, and existence. They also provide the nuclear opposites for the operation of sexual magic. The yang-yin idea is symbolically expressed in a famous diagram of the circle of *t'ai-chi* bisected by a sigmoid line, which shows the two black and white forces locked in an embrace of opposites.

A woman by virtue of her nature is a rich repository of yin in its most concentrated form, and when sexually aroused she is so irradiated with yin that her very presence can provide the living nexus for magical operations. At the time of orgasm she gives off a powerful pulse of psychic energy which ordinarily becomes diffused and lost. Taoism, and other sex-magical systems as well, recommend that the magician seal her mouth with his at this moment and quaff the effulgent draught, while at the same time by an interior absorbent process draw up the transmitted orgasmic impulse through his member. This is to be stored within his body.

Thus charged with power most adepts proceed on their own from this stage on, but there are others who go on to group rituals to increase their store. A single morsel is not enough for the purpose they seek, besides which women differ in their power-output, and it is not thought desirable to draw from a single source. By the second and third centuries AD there evolved in China a system for the collective Union of Breaths (*Ho Ch'i*) practiced by small groups of Taoists in communal sex rites.

In certain establishments at the new and full moon men and women came together for a feast of yang and yin in all its variety. The purpose of these exercises for the adept was not emission, which was regarded as a waste of precious substance that had to be conserved until the final phase, but retention. How he deferred emission was a simple matter of applying pressure to the perineum, which resulted in an arresting of the discharge. Modern physiologists explain it by saying that the pressure merely diverts the seminal stream into the bladder whence it is voided at the next urination, but according to Taoist teaching what is so rejected constitutes only the gross material semen, and not the subtle substance vitalised by yin impregnation which sends its puissant fumes to the brain and recharges the body.

The man now has within himself his own charge of yang fortified by a copious charge of yin and is ready for the procedure of creating the magical embryo within himself. Selecting a suitable time, to be decided by astrological factors, but preferably after midnight and at a time of year shortly following one of the solstices, he lies in a comfortable position on his back, turns his tongue up and inwards towards his throat as far as it will go and begins the exercises he has learned. He directs his *ch'i* or breath through the grand circuit, that is, through the chief plexuses of the body; then heating the sexual plexus with his supercharged breath-essence he unites yang and yin within himself in the region near the diaphragm. In a few hours he will become aware of the presence of the 'embryonic pearl' which constitutes the quintessence of yang and yin and the fruit of their partnership. This subtle embryo is fed on the pure nourishment provided by the breath-vitalised seminal essence imbued with yin energy. The embryo sends out a radiant force through the man's physical frame, growing and filling the interstices of his material body. That is the 'immortal body'.

The aim of Taoist sex magic as we have seen is the preservation or restoration of youth, the transformation of the body by revitalising the subtle energies, and the prolongation of life. In consequence of the teachings being widely spread throughout China and lasting over a thousand years through several dynasties and schools, the methods were extremely varied, some even more curious than that given in the above account. Let there be no doubt that there were always sober men, mainly of the Confucianist persuasion, who deplored these dubious pursuits, and had stern words as much for the depraved specimens who went in for these rites as for the wretched females who permitted the practice on their persons. The moral desirability of seeking supernormal powers, if such were possible, was also the subject of their censure.

Indeed, the feats ascribed to Taoist adepts are reminiscent of the Arabian Nights. They could tame wild animals with a glance; raise the dead; ride the clouds; become invisible; change their shape at will. They could make the 'director of destinies' erase their names from the 'book of death', for they claimed immortality. Stories are told of such adepts, who go through the motions of death and are duly buried, after which they spread the radiance of the embryonic pearl through the gross body and achieve the state of 'long-life-no-death', or immortality. As proof of their success their graves are opened after a certain time and no corpse is found, but only the shrouds and cerements and the ceremonial staff with which they were buried.

In India, sex magic is found in its most elaborate form in what is known as Tantrism, an ancient system whose origins are also not clear. Tantrism has a philosophy as rich as any in Hinduism, some of it with a sublime ethical content, but these higher principles are no more related to Tantrism in its sex-magical aspect than the aphorisms of Lao-Tzu are connected with Taoist communal orgies. This left-hand branch of Tantrism is alien to orthodox Hinduism and the pandit repudiates it. It is opposed to the Vedas, the original scriptures of Hinduism.

In common with Taoism there exists, according to Tantrik theory, a duality in the universe which, in this case, is theomorphised in a divine pair: the god Shiva and his consort Shakti. The dual principle girdles the universe and runs through it; it sustains the world and is the world, for whatever exists consists of the warp and woof made up of the duality of genders. A sexual element is inherent in all things. Man is male in relation to woman but he is also male-female within himself, and methods of union often parallel the Taoist system. There are also many variations of the renunciative technique which generates power by intensive temptation and stimulation of desire linked with self-control; different forms of sex practice in private, and of intercourse in group session.

In Tantrism the male-female union within man is bound up with the arousing of a vital power situated at the base of the spine known as the *kundalini*, which normally lies coiled and asleep. If accidentally or inadvertently awakened it can shake a person to the depths of his being, releasing a terrible force over which he has no control. It is sometimes referred to as the serpent of sexual fire, and complicated methods lasting over many years are required to be learned if one would arouse this force with safety. A special branch of yoga is devoted to it, intimately connected with *mantras* (magical sounds) and *pranayama* (breathing techniques).

Besides the physical body man possesses a subtle or astral body which is believed to come in contact with the physical body at certain points or psychic centres. These points and their interconnections are spread throughout the physical body like the framework of an invisible net. This net is susceptible to definite sound vibrations, and to definite breathing rhythms, and hence a knowledge of *mantras* and *pranayama* is required to activate a particular centre. There are certain vibratory *mantras*, especially those with a 'humming' sound, which are projected to the different parts of the body to make the psychic centres glow and by means of breath control to blow into flames the quiescent embers of the sexual fire force. The awakened *kundalini* then starts its journey through the successive centres of the subtle body until it joins the subtle centre at the top of the head. Various magical and psychical powers are supposed to result from this encounter if properly effected, but extremely dangerous results can follow from ignorant tampering with the force.

There is also a considerable demonological element in Tantrism, involving necromancy and conjuring up female demon-like beings or primeval hags, which is believed to have been introduced about AD 600 from the same mysterious Shambhala that has been mentioned above as the diffusion area for the Eastern systems of sex magic. Much information on this lore was lost in India as a result of the destruction of Tantrik monasteries by invaders, but most of the original tradition is still preserved in Tibet.

The Tibetan form of Tantrik mysticism owes its development to a school of esotericism founded by a master named Padma Sambhava, known to the Tibetans as the 'precious teacher'. He came, like so many others in this line of magical teaching, from a place called Urgyan in Central Asia, perhaps the Shambhala of legend, located somewhere near modern Afghanistan. Padma Sambhava visited India some time in AD 730 and taught at one of the Buddhist universities there, and on the invitation of the ruler of Tibet went to that country accompanied by his two wives and a chosen band of disciples. Here he had conflicts with demons and demonesses who opposed his attempts to displace them, but he himself established a tradition that degenerated in course of time into systems that became partly demonolatrous and, in some of their later phases, of atrocious sexuality. What contribution he personally made to the erotic rites is a matter of dispute but these may have acquired some elements from the existing 'native' religion known as Bon. His doctrines tinctured many of the other Tibetan systems and survived the reforms instituted by later teachers. Much of Tibetan ritual magic where it is connected with sexuality can be traced to his time if not indeed to him.

On the whole the Tibetan practices of this and other magical schools are associated with solitary meditation in caves; cemetery and corpse rites as a means of securing power over demons; sexuality with elemental beings ritually conjured up by thaumaturgy; the creation of an immortal 'vajra' (thunderbolt) body; acquisition of magical powers such as the ability to levitate, to influence the weather, to be immune to cold. This last relates to a mysterious power called *tummo*, a thermal energy from the seminal circuit that is distributed all over the body and raised by special breathing techniques to a high degree of heat. With proper practice it is possible so to charge the body with this internal heat as to make oneself entirely immune to the rigours of a Tibetan winter. A test for having mastered it is to sit naked on the shores of a frozen lake in midwinter with a fierce wind blowing and in the course of a single night to dry out at least three large sheets that have been dipped into the icy waters and wrapped around the body. The shamans of the Siberian steppe, who may have had direct access to the ancient springs of the magical tradition of Shambhala, were credited with similar powers and could sit without clothing in freezing cold out in the snow until it turned into steam with the heat that issued from their bodies.

The belief in the supernaturalism of sex seems to have entered effectively into the current of European thought with the Gnostics, a semi-Christian sect of theosophists who flourished in the early centuries of the present era in the eastern regions of the Mediterranean.

Gnosticism is actually not one but several sects lumped together by historians for the sake of convenience. Most of their literature is lost and the little that we have survives mainly in extracts found in the writings of the Church Fathers who quoted (and doubtless misquoted) from their works to provide material for their own fulminations against them.

Gnosticism had a complex philosophy whose doctrines have been traced to the ancient Egyptian mysteries, to Babylonian theogamy, Pythagorean numerology, Zoroastrian dualism, and Buddhist mysticism. It had an elaborate cosmology of its own concerning the origin of the world. From the fullness of the Divine Being there came forth or 'emanated' a series of cosmic entities known as 'Aeons' who represented the primeval forces connected with creation and with the various virtues and powers. The Aeon known as Demiurge was the one responsible for fashioning the material world.

The Aeons were often classed in what was known as a *syzygy*, or 'yoking' of pairs (again a hint of the word 'sex'). There were male Aeons and female Aeons, and they often remained wrapt in timeless embrace. Among the Aeons was Sophia (Wisdom) an archetypal female personifying the beauty of the universe and the wisdom underlying the redemptive process. She participated in the activities of the other Aeons at first but later renounced her allegiance to them and was condemned for 'refusing to do their mystery'.

Only fragmentary hints survive in the scraps of the ancient texts of what this 'mystery' was, but in its practical application it appears to have been one of several, and they seem to have covered both extremes of the moral gamut. Among the Gnostic practitioners there was a power-oriented asceticism and simplism, and also a left-hand trend formalised in rites of a perverse nature.

One of the Gnostics, Carpocrates (*c.* 115), said that God had implanted in man the burning sting of sexual desire to compel the human species to fornicate, for intercourse was pleasing to God. His followers obeyed the divine behest with ardour, making no distinction between the sexes. Another Gnostic leader, Valentinus (*d.* 165), pointed out that the copulating Aeons were exhausted by their sustained exertions on the world's behalf and had to be invigorated by intercourse on earth. The main sacrament of the Valentinians was a divine marriage in which the high priest and priestess would lie together, the congregation witnessing. Then, duty bound to the Demiurge they would turn to their partners and re-enact the sacred rite. Any form of intercourse was permitted, and the worse the better. The Church Fathers whose condemnation in this respect is not hard to understand, described the Gnostic Mass as 'monstrous, revolting abominations', and the whole Gnostic theory as the rankest heresy.

The influence of these sects has never entirely died out, and we find the embers flaring into sudden blaze in dozens of Neo-Gnostic fraternities throughout Christendom right down to modern times.

Following the Gnostics, the next landmark in the history of sex mysticism is to be found among a number of sects known by the generic name of Cathars, derived from the Greek word for 'pure'. The Cathar doctrine was a development of Gnosticism with a strong backing from Persian dualism. It spread via the Balkans and Bulgaria to western Europe, making its most zealous converts in northern Italy and southern France, and colouring the form of Christianity practised in those regions.

The Cathars themselves strongly opposed the lack of personal simplicity among church dignitaries, the stiff formalism of church worship, the greed, immorality and general corruption of the Church, and expressed their abhorrence of the whole ecclesiastical set-up. In turn the Cathars did not receive much charity at the hands of the church prelates, and were subjected to much bloody persecution. Their beliefs and practices were confused, perhaps intentionally, with those of other recalcitrants making the complex problem of Cathar doctrine still more difficult to sort out.

The Moorish occupation of Spain and the Crusades had introduced further eastern elements and the general consequence of these historic liaisons was the emergence of a new wave of thought that permeated European society, and through the popular poets and minstrels known as the troubadours changed the face of European literature. The medieval 'Courts of Love' that flourished in these same areas with their cult of unrequited passion, of virginity, of adultery, and sodomy, all to be savoured as a means of heightening the soul's intensity and ennobling passion by piety and perversion, were derived from the same stream.

According to the clerics the Cathar Mass was a sacrilegious travesty of the divine service, at which orgiastic rites took place with special emphasis on homosexuality. The sacred rite of marriage was condemned as sinful because it propagated other flesh and endlessly multiplied evil, but other forms of sexuality were encouraged. Whatever the truth may be, historians say that one of the Cathar sects, known as the Bogomils, 'God-beloved', have given their name to *bougre, bugger,* and other variant words for sodomist in a number of European languages.

A perusal of medieval church history would easily suggest to the reader that the transgression of chastity or the marriage vow, or even sexual aberration did not greatly trouble the ecclesiastical authorities. Nor were they unduly concerned at being the target of popular criticism. If it were only a matter of ridiculing or reviling the Church quite a number of popular movements and organisations would have been subject to persecution, but were not, although the Church did retaliate with ferocious cruelty whenever its authority was at stake, and almost always invoked infidelity and heresy as the point at issue.

The Templars, for instance, were an order of Christian knights whose ramifications extended all over Europe. They were also the richest, and they acknowledged only nominally their allegiance to the Church. Pope Clement V, fearful of the Brotherhood's wealth and power, conspired with Philip IV, king of France, to bring about their downfall. In a secretly-planned round-up the Templars were caught and imprisoned in their hundreds throughout Europe, charged with homosexuality and onanism, but especially with the worship of false gods, trampling on the Cross, and paying homage to a devilish idol named Baphomet. There were wholesale executions, starting with the burning alive of the Templar chief, Jacques de Molay, in March 1314. Before his martyrdom de Molay secretly entrusted commissions to four of his followers and to these four are traced the beginnings of some of the secret branches of the Rosicrucians, the Martinists, and other Illuminati.

The Church persecuted the Templars ostensibly for their unorthodoxy and not so much for their sexual misdemeanours. And this attitude seems to have been behind most of its condemnation of the prevailing practices to which it was opposed. The Feast of Fools, which used to take place on church premises, and other similar revels in which the bishops were mocked, continued for centuries with the full knowledge of the Church, and when they were finally stopped it was not primarily on grounds of licentiousness but because they were declared heretical, and derived from the Saturnalia and Bacchanalia, dedicated to pagan deities. The Dancing Mania in which many ecclesiastics themselves participated was finally condemned by the Church not as lewd, but as heretical. The Bull issued by Clement VI in 1394 against the sect of the Flagellants who went in procession through towns and villages beating themselves with whips and flails, condemned it as a 'heresy'.

Sexual desire was natural, and not always the subject of condemnation, and from the time of its promulgation the celibate vow for clerics was taken lightly all round. Many parish priests regarded as fair game for their sexual attentions the women among their flock. In some parishes this was so rampant that the townsfolk insisted that the clergy be permitted to keep mistresses so that their own homes might be secure from their depredations. A number of states imposed a tax called *cullagium*, which was virtually a licence for priests to keep concubines, and the establishments of some of the higher church dignitaries, certain popes not excluded, took on the dimensions of fair-sized harems.

Monastic houses and nunneries were hotbeds of vice, and the famous 16th-century Dutch scholar Erasmus, who was himself the illegitimate son of a monk, called them 'little better than brothels'. Prostitution was thought to be a necessary outlet for the libidinous male, and even St Thomas Aquinas said that it was expedient for the moral health, just as a sewer is essential to a palace if the whole place is not to smell. One notorious bishop took up the patronage of prostitutes as a financial sideline, and his pretty wards became known as the 'Winchester geese', providing him with a substantial profit.

The Church's interference in the activities of the various aberrant cults, therefore, did not rest primarily on moral grounds. It was not sex but the supernaturalism of sex that was the butt of their censure. It was the elevation of promiscuous sexuality to the status of a sacrament and the use of sex as a rite in some form of heretical religion.

Persons guilty of sexual misdemeanour were reprimanded, and where the misdemeanour was too scandalous, it could be written off for a financial consideration. Those accused of graver faults involving intellectual error – for instance, holding an opinion not in accord with the teachings of the Church – were tried by the ecclesiastical court. If found to be free from the taint of nonconformity they were 'relaxed' or sent to a secular court for trial. But where the heinous crime of heresy was suspected the awful machinery of the Inquisition was set in motion. The Church's concern, at least legalistically, was with dogma and not with immorality.

The sin of witchcraft lay therefore not in nude dancing, drunkenness or fornication, but in diablerie. The witch who put her husband into a trance and flew off with the hosts of Diana and Salome to the sabbat was condemned not for breaking the seventh commandment (against adultery) but the second (against worshipping other gods). The gravamen of the charge against witches included paying homage to Satan, trampling on the Cross, congress with demons, and the practice of maleficia. And these acts of maleficia were largely sexual, directed against the divine reproductive functions: inspiring illicit lust by means of charms and aphrodisiacs; preventing husband and wife from coming together; casting spells to make men impotent by 'knotting' the smaller cords of the sexual organs to prevent erection or emission; making women barren; causing pregnant women to abort; causing children of full term to be born dead; dedicating new-born children to Satan in a hurried, whispered rite of the black baptism.

The Church held in special odium those who linked sexual activity with diabolism, for then magical means were used in order to seduce women, and seduction then became a branch of sorcery and part of a larger conspiracy to inveigle men and women into the commonwealth of Lucifer.

An ordained priest is a specialist in ritualism, and when he forsakes the faith and dedicates himself to the infernal powers he is able to use his knowledge with far greater effectiveness than the secular diabolist. The history of satanism is remarkable for the number of renegade priests who officiated at ceremonies dedicated to Satan, and for the abominable punishments meted out to them when they were caught. A few of the more notorious cases, all taken from France, will illustrate this.

Louis Gaufridi, a priest of Provence, was horribly tortured, strangled, and burned at the stake in 1611 for having seduced a young convent girl. According to the records he used to 'breathe' upon her while in the confessional, and so clouded her mind that she was unaware of what she was doing. Having accomplished her moral corruption he seduced her spirit forcing her to participate in satanic rites at the witches' sabbat. She and a number of other nuns in the same convent became 'possessed' and suffered from violent convulsions and showed other signs of demonic influence.

In 1634 Urbain Grandier, French priest of Loudun, was tried by the ecclesiastical court and condemned to torture and the stake. His legs were bound between boards and the boards then hammered, blow by blow, till the blood spurted and the marrow oozed out. His cries of mortal agony could be heard from one end of the town to the other. Grandier was a very handsome man and he took full advantage of his natural charms to seduce a number of his female parishioners. The crime for which he suffered torture and death was not that of fornication but again that of magic and maleficia, causing demons to possess people, procuring the moral corruption of women, and thereafter making them participate in the worship of the Evil One.

Thirteen years later, in 1647, Father Boullé and several other priests were tried by the Church for having joined Madeleine Bavent and a group of nuns in the French convent of Louviers in obscene rites dedicated to the devil. They desecrated the Host, performed a marriage ceremony with a nun and the demon Dagon upon the altar, and committed other horrible acts of blasphemy. Father Boullé was tortured to death, along with a collaborating priest. The body of another priest who had started the satanic cult in the convent and had died before its discovery, was exhumed and publicly burned. Madeleine herself was imprisoned in a rat-infested dungeon and it has never been known how she died.

In 1733 the Jesuit priest, Jean-Baptiste Girard, stood trial before the Parlement d'Aix in France for sorcery. He was accused of seducing the young Catherine Cadière, then seventeen years old. He too used to 'breathe' upon her, and so inflame her mind that she would fall into a trance. Often his mere presence would give her the feeling that a finger was moving inside her and making her 'feel quite wet'. Adepts of the left hand were supposed to be proficient in inducing such orgasm from a distance. Girard would also flagellate her on the bare buttocks although this was not a matter of great concern since such 'disciplines', as they were known to church authorities, were commonly administered by priests to their flock. Finally, he was accused of being a sorcerer and of having bewitched the girl.

At the trial Girard was acquitted by a close margin in the voting of the judicial panel, his life being saved by the president casting a vote in his favour.

The life and activities of the Abbé Guibourg (*d.* 1683) are perhaps among the most extraordinary in the annals of diabolism, and were it not for the written evidence that exists to support the case, it would pass credibility. Here were all the nightmarish ingredients of sex and satanism at their worst; the sacrifice of living children to Astaroth, Asmodeus, and other pagan deities; sacramental Hosts being mixed with human flesh and menstrual blood; the use as holy sacraments of fluids ejected from the body. A naked woman was made to lie with legs apart upon a table to form an altar, a candle placed on her belly and her private orifice used as a ciborium for the Host. There were incredible variations of the Black Mass called Semen Mass and Faeces Mass, culminating in an enactment of such sacrilege that it could only occur to a mind benumbed to any decent human instincts, or utterly unhinged from long association with the worst aspects of depravity.

The name of this psychopath is linked with another notorious diabolist, Madame Deshayes, popularly known as La Voisin, and she again was only a cog in a great machinery of sorcery and vice that extended through 18th-century French society. The principal significance of this affair was the number of priests who were mixed up with diabolism and sex, in forms which included necrophilia and cannibalism involving, it was alleged, the ritual sacrifice of over 2,500 children. When the Deshayes affair was finally uncovered through the tireless exertions of an incorruptible police officer, Nicholas de la Reynie, the disclosures were so scandalous and implicated so many prominent personages that Louis XIV ordered the investigations to be brought to an end and some of the records destroyed. His own favourite Madame de Montespan was involved and so were many of the highest in the land. Some of the influential nobles, dukes and marquises among them, were given a chance to get out of the country, but over 300 people were imprisoned, thirty-four banished and more than thirty sentenced to death. Obviously for these lords and ladies and the dozens of priests concerned, it was not the easily obtainable thrill of sex that fascinated them but the forbidden ventures into diabolism, the allure of increased power, the clandestine participation in ceremonies where revulsion and guilt added their own sting of perverse delight to the pleasure of sexual indulgence.

To bring the French line of diabolists up to date three names should be mentioned. First, Pierre Vintras (*d.* 1875), who founded a Neo-Gnostic rite known after him as the Vintrasian Mass. His following included priests, scholars, and distinguished professional men. There were nude rites, blood-drinking, and sexual communion before an altar where all forms of sex were enacted by the worshippers. The cult symbols were the satanic goat, the *linga* or phallic symbol of the god Shiva, and blood-stained lilies representing virtue debauched. When his sect received official censure from the Vatican, Vintras with supreme aplomb threatened to excommunicate the Pope.

After Vintras's death his mission in satanism was carried on by Joseph-Antoine Boullan (*d.* 1893), abbé and black magician, a man of high intellectual distinction and deeply versed in supernatural lore. Boullan held that the Fall was due to forbidden love and hence Redemption was to be achieved through sacramental sexuality. As a priest he could consecrate Hosts and did so with his own brand of ritual, mixing the wafers with his own feces and administering them to his flock 'to fertilise the soul'. His cult was dedicated entirely to sex magic but he did not confine the act to the physical body on the earthly plane. He gave special instructions to a few selected disciples on methods of performing intercourse with their own astral and other astral bodies on the etheric planes.

When Boullan fell foul of another black magician a celebrated 'battle of sorcerers' took place on the astral level. Malignant currents and countercurrents were discharged, curses hurled across the ether and elemental forces despatched by both sides. Boullan apparently got the worst of the psychic encounter; he began to complain of blows received from invisible fists, saw strange shapes and heard ominous sounds, and died soon after in a sudden agonising seizure.

The last of the unholy triumvirate was the Abbé Haecke (*d.* 1912), apostate priest and devil worshipper who reputedly had the soles of his feet tattooed with crosses so that he might have the constant satisfaction of trampling upon the hated symbol of the Church. His satanic society lacked none of the disgusting sexual features of the others we have mentioned. Perhaps not so strangely he was a man afraid of the dark and would often wake up at night and scream in terror and start putting on the lights in the house, and shouting imprecations against God when his self composure returned. He was the model for the sinister Canon Docre in Huysmans's celebrated novel *La Bas.*

In other parts of Europe various types of sex supernaturalism were also being promulgated. One form of it is traceable to a man far removed from the ambit of diabolism and he himself, it must be emphasised, was in no way responsible for the course it took. The man was Emanuel Swedenborg (*d.* 1772), a person of the noblest principles and of extraordinary intellectual attainments. The son of a bishop, he received the best possible education in the liberal arts and sciences, travelled widely in Europe, and for his contribution to learning was ennobled by his monarch.

Swedenborg wrote learnedly and with authority on astronomy, geology, palaeontology, anatomy, brain-physiology, economics, tides, docks, sluices, saltworks, military engineering, calculus, longitude, decimal measures, mining, smelting, metallurgy. He invented the ear-trumpet, a machine-gun that could fire seventy shots a minute, an improved type of steam-engine, an airpump, and made various improvements on other existing inventions. He was by no means a hare-brained mystic.

At the age of fifty-five, when at the height of his fame, he started having visions, and abandoned the pursuit of material wisdom. The sciences, he felt, contributed nothing to salvation, but rather distorted ideas and confused the mind. He announced that he was in touch with the heavenly spheres. The Lord Himself, he declared, 'opened to my sight the view of the spiritual world'. He claimed to have visited the heavens and the hells, and wrote down his apocalyptic visions in a series of inspired works which totalled forty volumes.

All things experienced by the senses, according to Swedenborg, were symbols of a supernatural reality. Every material thing had a spiritual cause that could not be discerned by physical sight. There was a close relationship between a thing done on the material plane and its causes or consequences in the non-material sphere. One of his works deals with the spiritual meaning of those mysterious early books of the Bible, Genesis and Exodus, and part of his revelation is concerned with the sexes and their significance in the next world, a matter that has exercised thinkers and prophets of all ages.

Is there sex in the other world? The question often crops up in discussions about life after death, and there are as usual a plethora of theories. In primitive societies the wives and concubines of the chief of the tribe used to be sacrificed at his graveside so that they might continue to minister to his sexual needs in the next world. According to this belief, then, there was sex on the other side. Other more sophisticated systems also preserve relics of this view. The Hindu paradise (there are several) has its quota of beauteous nymphs who will provide for the needs of those destined for the land of the blest. The Muslim paradise is filled with houris, virgins who will delight the eye with their beauty and fill the chambers of paradise with their perfume.

Spiritualists generally hold that men and women cast off the appurtenances of sex after death, and that while they may retain their own form for a time they do not have sexual intercourse. On the whole sex is regarded in most advanced religious systems as part of the material world, to be abandoned when we leave the mortal plane, so that if there is 'propagation' over there it will be by some other mode. Even among the Muslims there have been a few philosophers who have had a bad conscience about the houris and have explained these creatures as representing the virtues that dwell in heaven in all their virgin purity and imbue man with their love and goodness. Jesus specifically said that in heaven there would be no marriage or giving in marriage.

In Swedenborg's philosophy the union of man and woman is one of the primary purposes of creation. Every person has a 'spiritual counterpart', whom he should seek to meet on earth. The counterparts having met, should unite. This should be in seemly intercourse, for sex has its proper channels. Sodomy and sexual perversion were matters of extreme abhorrence in the spiritual world, and those guilty of such sins received infernal torments 'so dire they can scarcely be described'. If for any reason a person could not find his counterpart while on earth he would meet her in heaven, although in heaven no actual sexual union took place. Connected with this doctrine was one of 'internal respiration', and although Swedenborg never made it clear what this was, the idea was elaborated by his disciples along their own lines of interpretation.

When Swedenborg died in 1772 he had a small and zealous following who, in the course of a few decades, spread the teachings to the rest of Europe, whence it reached America. In 1844 a young man of eighteen named Andrew Jackson Davis, a clairvoyant and mystic, claimed that Swedenborg appeared to him in a vision and told him that he had a mission for mankind. The son of a drunkard father and an illiterate mother, and himself a cobbler by trade, Davis had had no proper education. His father knew about the 'voices' that spoke to the lad, and on the advice of one of these intimations from the other world he moved with his family to Poughkeepsie in New York State. Here young Davis composed some extraordinary works on cosmic evolution while in a trance state. Under the inspiration of the spiritual-counterpart teachings Davis subsequently acquired a rather lax view of marriage and lived with a married woman, and scandalised his flock.

His best known disciple was Thomas Lake Harris, an Englishman who was to take the counterpart doctrine and the breathing system of Swedenborg and produce an amalgam of his own. Harris was born in 1823 at Fenny Stratford in Buckinghamshire, and when five years of age was taken to America by his parents. Like Davis he tended to have visions and hear spirit voices. He met and was attracted to Davis and learned all the older man had to teach, but eventually broke away from the Poughkeepsie seer and ventured out on his own.

Harris established a number of communities where a kind of socialism was practised, including the sharing of wives. He too wrote a book explaining the Bible in its 'celestial' sense as Swedenborg had explained it in its spiritual sense. God was a Dual-Unit, a Two-in-One and man, although he reflected this androgynous condition, was basically incomplete, and could only achieve wholeness by finding and uniting with his spiritual counterpart. Harris claimed to have his immortal bride in heaven, but he found the marks of her in a succession of women whom he took as his temporary partners in accordance with his teachings. Interwoven with this doctrine of counterparts was a theory of 'internal respiration', that involved a special kind of breathing through which the divine effluvium was drawn into the body by 'arch-natural' (his term for 'supernatural') means, and revitalised and reinvigorated body, soul, and spirit. By means of this technique, he claimed that disease could be banished and death itself postponed indefinitely. Harris himself lived to be more than eighty. Towards the end his followers were numbered in thousands and included men and women from all walks of life and all strata of society. Many of them gave him all their wealth on joining his sect.

Perhaps the most remarkable among his disciples was a strange Scotsman named Laurence Oliphant, who was the son of the Chief Justice of Ceylon, the nephew of the Director and Chairman of the East India Company, and the cousin of Margaret Oliphant, a famous writer in her day and author of over one hundred and twenty-five books. Laurence himself was regarded as one of the ten best writers of his time. He was a brilliant conversationalist, irresistibly attractive to the opposite sex, and the darling of his social circle, which was one of the most exclusive in England. He was also a man of action, travelled from Japan to Nicaragua, from Lapland to Singapore, and served as special correspondent to *The Times*, covering the Crimean War and other historic events.

Oliphant first met Harris in 1860 and by 1864 was completely under his spell. When Oliphant was elected to Parliament his guru ordered him not to take an active part in the proceedings of the House and during the entire period of his parliamentary life Oliphant never said a word in the House. He was summoned to one of the Harris colonies where he was given menial tasks like cleaning out the cattle sheds and stables. His sleeping quarters were in a cattle loft and his bed a row of empty orange-boxes. He was made to work alone and in silence and the food he received was far from adequate. In winter he slogged in the open with just enough clothing to keep him from freezing, and his hands and feet were almost permanently numb. Yet he found that this experience brought him 'something indescribable and more wonderful than all the flesh-pots of a thousand Egypts'. His mother, the elegant and highly cultured Lady Oliphant, joined her son and was put to work washing dishes, cleaning and mending for the household, and hoeing in the fields. She was not permitted to talk to her son although mother and son had always been very closely bound by ties of affection.

After two years Oliphant was finally allowed to return to normal social life and while in London he met and married the beautiful Alice Le Strange. Harris reluctantly agreed to the union but totally prohibited sexual intercourse. The ban was said to have been maintained by this remarkable pair for twelve years. Husband and wife went to America after the wedding and Harris finding the marks of his 'counterpart' in the beautiful bride immediately separated the couple.

Oliphant was greatly attached to his mother and it

was only after she had been utterly broken in body and spirit and died of cancer in 1881 that the evil spell was broken and Oliphant returned to civilisation. But it soon became clear from Oliphant's behaviour that he was permanently changed by the teachings of Harris. The search for the counterpart never left him: internal respiration was to haunt him for the rest of his days. He and his wife became inspired by missionary zeal and settled in Haifa, Palestine, to preach their own version of Harrisite mysticism, which was the worship of a bisexual God who can be approached by man only through sex.

The Oliphants called their brand of mysticism *sympneumata*, or 'co-breathing', and wrote a book about it. They advocated a technique which combined a unified mystical breathing-together while in sexual union. It is not easy to understand, and has been variously described as 'mystical masturbation', 'occult homosexualism', and 'religious sensuality'. Perhaps it did have a profounder meaning; Oliphant's friend, General Gordon, to whom he once read extracts, said that 'it was all in the Bible though few would recognise it'. In order to help her Arab converts to learn the technique correctly Mrs Oliphant, one of the most refined women of England, used to give them practical instruction in pursuance of her holy mission, but she found the demonstration a great trial as many of her converts were dirty and degraded.

After his wife's death Oliphant carried on his work alone, teaching his disciples the technique of 'auto-erotic mysticism', 'redemption through sex', and other profound sexual secrets. The National Vigilance

Society had in the meantime got wind of the goings on of this eccentric propagandist for redemption through sex, but before anything could be done Oliphant died and the results of their investigations were never made public.

Perhaps the climax of these mystical antics was reached in the cult founded by a woman of many aliases, who after a nomadic career in theosophy, spiritualism, cartomancy, and contact with other-world denizens through opium trances, found her soul-mate in the person of one Frank Dutton Jackson, and married him. Mrs Editha Anna Jackson was a woman of huge proportions and with a personality of overwhelming power, while her husband was a puny fellow seventeen years younger. In their flat in London they evolved certain rites of sex magic in which Jackson, with his wife assisting, participated in ceremonial acts of intercourse with young girls, supposedly utilising the powers engendered by titillation and stimulation of the sexual apparatus for magical ends. Every known device was brought into play. At their subsequent trial the full facts were never put on record; often the court had to be cleared to prevent the sordid details from being made public. The *Lancet* found some of the disclosures 'too revolting to relate'.

From the middle of the last century the cults devoted to mysticism in which sex played a part could be numbered by the score both in Europe and America. They usually claimed an ancient Egyptian, Eastern, Rosicrucian, or other similar ancestry, and took themselves very seriously. They were particular about membership, and bound their adherents to the strictest oaths of secrecy, perhaps as much to keep their activities from the police as to preserve their mysteries. It seemed that few of those who studied the mystic arts could resist the urge to set up their own brand of some past religion, and most of them offered the blueprint for a new dispensation for mankind, dedicated to human regeneration through the inner forces, especially sexual.

Dr P. B. Randolph (*d.* 1875), well-known American occultist and alleged friend of Lincoln, combined a form of mysticism imported from Syria with the stimulation of inner powers. He wrote a controversial book on sex magic and for that or some other connected reason was thought to have been murdered, though it was also rumoured that he may have committed suicide. His successors spoke of a mysterious force, known to the ancients and passed down the ages through a line of adepts to our own day, which was capable of transforming the world.

That sex was indeed a force that is measurable, that discharges currents, that has magnetic and other physical properties, was seriously believed by a number of these exponents. We live, they said, in a sea of invisible impulses, something like the ether of 19th-century physics, but having a vibrant and rampageous energy that manifests in the animal kingdom as sex. In man this sexual energy can be stepped up to greater heights by methods known only to a few and jealously guarded by them. Like defloration, orgasm was thought to deliver a shock of high voltage to the etheric body, and the impact of this charge could be utilised, if properly 'wired'.

Not all who subscribed to such ideas were cranks, for some were sober men with scientific training. Perhaps the most notable among them was Dr Wilhelm Reich (*d.* 1957), Austrian-born scientist of phenomenal learning, who settled in America. In his book on the function of the orgasm Reich stated that the perfect orgasm was a rarity and its lack was responsible for our inhibitions. He attributed the rise of Hitler to sexual frustration of this kind, and damned the Nazis as orgastically impotent. He said that sexual energy could be improved by proper breathing techniques, which would change the shallow, unsatisfactory orgasms of the average man to a satisfactory kind that would transform the psyche. Reich regarded sexual energy as only one form of what he called *orgone*, a universal electric-magnetic-etheric force which permeates all nature, and is as powerful as atomic energy although antagonistic to it. He carried out a number of strange experiments with machines of his own invention and was finally arrested by the US authorities for reasons that are still not clear. He died in prison. It has been suggested from a perusal of his extant notes that he may have been on the track of a hitherto unknown force. One of his defenders said that his findings were 'factual, demonstrable, irrefutable, as were those of Galileo'.

If not the greatest, certainly the best known of the modern magicians was Aleister Crowley, an inspired dilettante who achieved distinction in most of the things that caught his fancy, from chess to mountaineering. He went through the substantial fortune inherited from his brewer father, as well as other large sums of money he earned, or acquired through his disciples, most of it spent on the theory and practice of 'magick' (as he insisted on spelling the word), the one art to which he was seriously dedicated, and to which he remained faithful throughout his long and eventful life.

He seems to have gathered in his hands the clues to most of the arcane knowledge of the past, and his writings covered practically every branch of the subject, but his main contribution was to goety, or black magic, which he learned from schools of both eastern and western occultism. His brand of magic is full of danger for the unwary and heady wine even for the adept. It is of course largely sexual in character, for he was the unequivocal champion of the left-hand path.

Crowley's strict upbringing in a rigidly fundamentalist Christian sect gave him an exceptional mastery of the Bible, but the characters after his heart were the symbolical figures accursed in the Book of Revelation: the Great Whore, the Dragon, the False Prophet, Jezebel, and the Woman arrayed in scarlet, and he himself took the title of the Great Beast after another ally of the Adversary mentioned in the same book. He once said that early in life God and Satan had struggled for his soul and he was never sure who won. But there was no doubt whom he served. He announced the end of the epoch of Jesus, and the inauguration of the age of Horus and the beginning of Crowleyanity, the new religion of the age. As its leader he devoted his talents as a poet and fine craftsman with words to hymns to pagan deities and invocations to the dark powers, and to the composition of Neo-Gnostic masses not devoid of blasphemy. Like others of similar persuasion he made elixirs of his semen and said his excretions were sacred.

Crowley regarded sex as an 'opus', a magical act or sacred 'working', and advocated sexuality in all its aspects. One of his rites in honour of the pagan gods prescribed (with what seriousness one could never be sure with him) the dismemberment or flaying of a girl after she was violated. Among his grimoires or magical textbooks is the *Liber Samekh* which includes a rite involving self-abuse. He had a succession of counterparts whom he referred to as his 'scarlet women', and if the exigencies of the magical occasion demanded a homosexual act he was equal to it with his male disciples.

Crowley held that a monogamous relationship was likely to cause spiritual malnutrition, since different women provided their own kind of nourishment necessary for male welfare. He himself had intimate relations with women of all kinds and nationalities: English, French, and other Europeans, Americans, Egyptians, Indians, Negroes, Burmese, Chinese, Nepali. He savoured of virgins and prostitutes, married women and spinsters. In his view it was necessary for a start to have experience of about a thousand women chosen from eighty to a hundred races and sub-races. He had a low opinion of women in general (he felt they should be made public property!) and of white women in particular, for he found them either vicious or intellectual in their approach to sexual matters.

A scandalised society, with some justification, denounced Crowley as one of the most infamous men of his age, but the mood of outrage has passed, and today, if he cannot be said to be coming into his own, he is at any rate being regarded as an articulate spokesman for a viewpoint that deserves to be given a hearing if we would understand the paradox of human nature in all its unbelievable variety.

Further Reading

Calverton, V. F., *et al.*, *Sex in Civilisation*, Allen & Unwin, London, 1929

Cavendish, Richard, *The Black Arts*, Routledge & Kegan Paul, London, 1967

Cutner, H., *A Short History of Sex Worship*, Watts, London, 1940

Denomy, A., *The Heresy of Courtly Love*, D. X. McMullen, New York, 1947

Dulaure, J. A., *The Gods of Generation*, Panurge Press, New York, edition of 1930

Evans-Wentz, W. Y. (ed.), *Tibetan Yoga and Secret Doctrines*, Oxford University Press, 2nd edition, 1958

Goldberg, B. Z., *The Sacred Fire: The Story of Sex in Religion*, Jarrolds, London, 1931

van Gulik, R. R., *Sexual Life in Ancient China*, E. J. Brill, Leiden, 1961

Laurent, E., & Nagour P., *Magica Sexualis*, Falstaff Press, New York, 1934

Licht, Hans, *Sexual Life in Ancient Greece*, Routledge & Kegan Paul, London, 1932

Mead, G. R. S., *Fragments of a Faith Forgotten: The Gnostics*, University Books, New York, edition of 1960

Partridge, Burgo, *A History of Orgies*, Spring Books, London, 1964

Rhodes, H. T. F., *The Satanic Mass*, Rider & Co, 1954

Runciman, S, *The Medieval Manichee*, Cambridge University Press, 1955

Strachey, R. C., *Religious Fanaticism*, Faber, London, 1928

Summers, Montague (ed.), *Demonality or Incubi and Succubi* (by Sinistrari), Fortune Press, London, 1927

Summers, Montague (ed.), *Malleus Maleficarum*, Pushkin Press, 1928

Symonds, John, *The Magic of Aleister Crowley*, Frederick Muller, London, 1958

Taylor, G. Rattray, *Sex in History*, Thames and Hudson, London, 1959

Walker, Benjamin, *Hindu World*, Allen & Unwin, 1968

ABOUT THE AUTHOR

Benjamin Walker, an Indian, was educated in Calcutta. Poet, historian, and traveller, he was formerly joint editor of the quarterly *Asia*, published in Saigon, and was for ten years a diplomat in the Indian Foreign Service. He is the author of *Persian Pageant* and *Angkor Empire*, and also of a two-volume encyclopedia, the first of its kind, entitled *Hindu World*. He is an authority on occultism and a contributor to *Man, Myth & Magic*, and is now completing a comprehensive survey of the whole field of the occult, East and West. He lives in Teddington, Middlesex, with his English wife.

ACKNOWLEDGMENTS

We are grateful to the following for permission to use copyright prints and photographs:

Chris Barker, 1; Camera Press London, 8; Peter Larson—Rex Features Ltd, 2; Mansell Collection, 4; Axel Poignant, 7; Prof. E. Evans Pritchard, 6; Radio Times Hulton Picture Library, 5.